THE INVINCIBLES
TEAM ONE

BOOK THREE

GRINDED

USA TODAY BESTSELLING AUTHOR
HEATHER SLADE

GRINDED
© 2020 Heather Slade

All rights reserved. No part of this book may be used or reproduced in any manner whatsoever without written permission, except in the case of brief quotations embodied in critical articles and reviews.

This book is a work of fiction. The names, characters, places and incidents are products of the writer's imagination or have been used fictitiously and are not to be construed as real. Any resemblance to persons, living or dead, actual events, locale or organizations is entirely coincidental.

979-8-88649-136-4

grinded
/grahynd/
verb
worn smoothed,
or sharpened

MORE FROM AUTHOR HEATHER SLADE

BUTLER RANCH
Kade's Worth
Brodie's Promise
Maddox's Truce
Naughton's Secret
Mercer's Vow
Kade's Return
Butler Ranch Christmas

WICKED WINEMAKERS
FIRST LABEL
Brix's Bid
Ridge's Release
Press' Passion
Zin's Sins
Tryst's Temptation

WICKED WINEMAKERS
SECOND LABEL
Beau's Beloved
Coming Soon:
Cru's Crush
Bones' Bliss
Snapper's Seduction
Kick's Kiss

ROARING FORK RANCH
Coming Soon:
Roaring Fork Wrangler
Roaring Fork Roughstock
Roaring Fork Rockstar
Roaring Fork Rooker
Roaring Fork Bridger

THE ROYAL AGENTS
OF MI6
Make Me Shiver
Drive Me Wilder
Feel My Pinch
Chase My Shadow
Find My Angel

K19 SECURITY
SOLUTIONS TEAM ONE
Razor's Edge
Gunner's Redemption
Mistletoe's Magic
Mantis' Desire
Dutch's Salvation

K19 SECURITY
SOLUTIONS TEAM TWO
Striker's Choice
Monk's Fire
Halo's Oath
Tackle's Honor
Onyx's Awakening

K19 SHADOW OPERATIONS
TEAM ONE
Code Name: Ranger
Code Name: Diesel
Code Name: Wasp
Code Name: Cowboy
Code Name: Mayhem

K19 ALLIED INTELLIGENCE
TEAM ONE
Code Name: Ares
Code Name: Cayman
Code Name: Poseidon
Code Name: Zeppelin
Code Name: Magnet

K19 ALLIED INTELLIGENCE
TEAM TWO
Coming Soon:
Code Name: Puck
Code Name: Michelangelo
Code Name: Typhon
Code Name: Hornet
Code Name: Reaper

PROTECTORS
UNDERCOVER
Undercover Agent
Undercover Emissary
Coming Soon:
Undercover Savior
Undercover Infidel
Undercover Assassin

THE INVINCIBLES
TEAM ONE
Decked
Edged
Grinded
Riled
Smoked

THE INVINCIBLES
TEAM TWO
Bucked
Irished
Sainted
Hammered
Ripped

THE UNSTOPPABLES
TEAM ONE
Furied
Married

COWBOYS OF
CRESTED BUTTE
A Cowboy Falls
A Cowboy's Dance
A Cowboy's Kiss
A Cowboy Stays
A Cowboy Wins

Table of Contents

Prologue

Grinder

It had been ten years since it last snowed in the hills outside of Austin, Texas. *Ten years.* It had also been ten years since I first met Pia Deltetto—the woman I believed might one day be my wife, the mother of my children.

I'd lived a lot of life in the years between then and now. Most of which I'd prefer to forget. There were days, weeks, even months when I wished I could forget Pia too, but she was too stubborn to let me. Her fiery spirit would force itself out of my subconscious until she was once again the star of my dreams—both awake and asleep.

Invariably, that meant I'd soon hear from her, as though my own spirit was connected to hers no matter where we were in the world.

I was on my way to see Pia now, traveling to the airport on this cold-as-hell night. It would take me fifteen hours to get to Florence, Italy. By the time I reached Tuscany, it would be Christmas.

Perhaps her gift to me would be one of forgiveness, although I knew, in my heart, that would be too much to ask for.

1

Grinder
Ten Years Ago
Val d'Orcia, Italy

"It's two months. You'll survive," my older sister, Lily, said the day my parents and I left London and traveled to Tuscany. Easy for her to say since she didn't have to spend her summer holiday in a country where she didn't know a soul.

I sighed and dropped my bags in what would be my bedroom, my sanctuary, my escape for the next sixty-five days. I flung myself on the bed, put my hands under my head, and looked out the window.

The place where my parents and I were staying, sat on the edge of the estate and winery known as *Antica Cascina dei Conti di Valentini*—which translated to "Ancient Farmhouse of the Counts of Valentini." Looking out at the much newer and larger villa in the distance, my guess was we were staying in the estate's namesake.

I pulled a book out of my travel bag and rested my head on the pillow that felt as old as the farmhouse. I wasn't through the first chapter when I heard a female laughing outside the window.

I rolled out of bed and caught a glimpse of a girl more beautiful than any I'd ever seen. She was walking backward in the open field adjacent to the house.

A teenage boy followed, who she alternately ran from and then turned around and teased, laughing all the while. I was transfixed, unable to tear my eyes away even when she caught me spying on them from the window and waved. Only when the guy she was with turned, followed her line of sight, and flipped me off, did I retreat back to my bed.

I picked up my book, but set it back down when I realized I'd read several paragraphs and didn't retain a word. I closed my eyes and pictured her. Who was she? I had to find out.

It was several days before I saw her again. I'd reached the point where I doubted I would.

On this particular morning, my father begged off taking my mum to the open-air market in the local village, so she recruited me. I didn't complain. In fact, I welcomed the change of scenery.

As I leaned my torso against the car, I felt her before I saw her. I slowly turned, and there she was, standing next to a fountain. A bouquet of flowers dangled in her hand, the petals brushing the cobblestones beneath her feet.

"Buongiorno," she said, raising her free hand.

"Buongiorno." I raised my hand too. As she walked closer, I let my eyes drift from her waist-length dark hair to her warm brown eyes, her pretty neck, her narrow waist, and her long legs. I tried to keep my eyes from lingering too long on the way her boobs strained the fabric of her dress, or on how the pale blue of it made her smooth skin appear the color of honey.

"You like to look," she said, standing less than a foot from me. "From windows, as I walk toward you…"

"It's hard not to. You're very beautiful."

Her eyes scrunched and she cocked her head. "Beautiful?"

"Is there something wrong with being beautiful?"

She shrugged her shoulders. "There is more to see in a woman than her beauty."

"I agree."

She smiled. "Tell me what else you see."

"You like to laugh."

"*Sì.*"

"You're romantic."

She raised a brow.

I looked her up and down a second time, which didn't appear to bother her. "Your dress. The way you carry your flowers as though you've almost forgotten they're in your hand because your mind is in the clouds instead."

She came closer and leaned against the car. The scent of her overwhelmed me.

"And you smell bloody fantastic."

She bent at the waist and laughed just like she had the first time I saw her walking in the field. I loved the sound of it.

"Oh, good. Miles, I'm so happy you've finally met Pia," I heard my mum say. She thrust the bags of bread, vegetables, and other purchases into my arms and then cheek-kissed the woman next to me.

"I've heard so much about you, *Mylos,*" Pia said, using the Italian version of my name while brushing her shoulder against mine.

I couldn't help but glare in my mother's direction.

"All good, Miles," she said, taking one of the bags from my arms and tossing it in the car through the open window. "We're just heading back. Can we give you a lift, Pia?"

"*Grazie,* but I have a few more errands in the village."

"We could wait," I blurted at the same moment a guy approached, put his arm around Pia's waist, and leaned into her.

"*Ti stavo cercando, bella.*"

"I haven't been hiding, Paolo."

"*Andiamo.*" He grabbed the hand that held her flowers.

"*Arrivederci, Signora* Stone, Mylos.*"

"Well, that was rude." My mum huffed and grabbed the rest of her purchases from my arms and put them in the car through the window like she had the other.

I watched as Pia walked away with Paolo, realizing now he was the same guy I saw her with from my window, the one who'd flipped me off. I was bothered less by his rudeness than the idea the arsehole was her boyfriend.

My mum prattled on all the while I drove back to the farmhouse. I learned that Pia, who was my age, was the only daughter of Giovanni Deltetto and his wife,

Countess Maria. She had no idea why Pia's mother was a countess and her father wasn't a count, nor did she know who Count Valentini was other than that the estate named for him had been in their family for several generations.

Later, as we sat on the *terrazza* having just finished another brilliant dinner prepared by my mum, who'd embraced Mediterranean cuisine in a way she never had with traditional English fare, we heard loud voices coming from the direction of the hilltop villa.

"Oh, dear," she muttered, getting up to clear the dishes and take them inside. My father joined her, but I didn't.

I walked down the steps to the lawn and looked toward the sound of the voices. I couldn't make out the exact words, but I could tell that a male and female were in a heated argument. I wasn't certain the female's voice was Pia's, but it sounded like it could be.

When the shouting died down, I went inside, where I found my parents sitting at the table in the kitchen.

"Everything all right?"

"Your mum finds this somewhat…disconcerting."

I nodded, wondering—not for the first time—what they were thinking when they'd decided to rent a place in Italy for an entire summer holiday. I mean, what had they expected?

The following week, when my mum appeared recovered from the excitement of a few days prior, I volunteered to take her into the village. I suppose part of me hoped to run into Pia again, given I hadn't seen her since the day we met.

Rather than waiting at the car, this time, I walked through the market after both my parents, since Dad had also volunteered to ride along.

"Where did she learn this?" I asked my father as we both stood stunned, watching my mum haggle with the street vendors. "I didn't even know she spoke Italian."

"She doesn't."

"Clearly, she—"

He shook his head. "Pia coached her. If you pay attention, you'll notice she repeats the same phrases again and again. I don't know the exact translation, but I believe she's calling them crazy for asking for so much money."

Now that he mentioned it, I had heard her say the word *pazzo*, which meant crazy, although I was fairly certain she was using it in the wrong context.

I turned around and looked out at the fountain that sat in the middle of the public square. I sighed, wishing for just one glimpse of the girl I couldn't stop thinking about.

Someone else caught my eye instead. *Paolo.* I squinted and took a second and third look just to confirm the girl he was with, the one he had his arm around, the one whose neck he just nuzzled, was absolutely not Pia.

This had to mean I'd been right when I guessed it was them arguing that night on the hilltop. It also had to mean they'd broken up.

When I saw him look over, I spun around so my back was to him.

"What's this?" asked my dad when my expression of bored disinterest transformed into a smile I couldn't contain.

"Nothing…Think Mum is ready to head back?"

My father shook his head and motioned over to where she was embroiled in an argument with the fishmonger as heated as the one we overheard that had sent her into such a tizzy.

Three more days passed before I finally saw Pia again.

I spent as much time as I could outside, taking in the lush, rolling hillsides covered in vineyards and orchards. Val d'Orcia, where the estate was located, was arguably the most beautiful stretch of Tuscan countryside in existence, and the sandstone villa and accompanying winery was as picture-perfect as the landscape. If I were to close my eyes and imagine what a quintessential view of Italy might be, even before visiting, this was exactly what I would've conjured.

While I traipsed along the rows and rows of grapevines, I'd stopped short of knocking on the door of the villa and asking for her. This morning I woke determined to talk to her.

I walked up the hillside, certain I felt the eyes of the vineyard workers settle on me as I trudged by. Was it my imagination that they were snickering?

"Tu chi sei?" I heard a voice ask when I reached the *terrazza* that led to the villa's front door.

"I'm Miles. My parents and I…"

"I know who you are. What do you want?"

If he knew who I was, why had he asked?

"Um…is Pia home? I'd like to speak with her."

"No." He waved his hand as though he was dismissing me.

As I crept away, I knew it hadn't been my imagination earlier when I wondered if the workers were snickering. They definitely had been, only not quite as loudly as they were now.

I was partway down the hill when I thought I heard someone calling my name. I turned around, and Pia was running toward me.

"Mylos, wait! I'm sorry about my father," she said, out of breath from trying to catch me. "He can be *uno stronzo arogante*."

"It's okay. I shouldn't have intruded."

"It isn't you…He's just protective." She put her arm through mine, and we continued down the hillside. "How are you, Mylos?"

"I'm fine, but I was worried about you."

Pia stopped walking and studied me. "Why?"

"Your breakup with Paolo. I thought maybe you—"

"Paolo and I didn't break up. What are you talking about?"

"You know. The argument. And then I saw him a couple of days ago."

She cocked her head. "A couple of days ago? That's impossible. Paolo is in Veneto."

"Unless he has a twin brother, he wasn't in Veneto three days ago. I saw him."

Pia's eyes scrunched. "Where did you see him?"

"I took my mum to the market, and he was there with…someone."

Her hands went to her hips. "Someone? What does that mean…*someone*?"

I kept walking. "Never mind."

"No. You said you saw Paolo with *someone*. Tell me what you meant. You saw him with a woman?"

I shook my head and continued walking. "My mistake. Like you said, Paolo is in Veneto. It was just someone who looked like him."

"*Mylos!*" she shouted after me, but I didn't stop. This was the first and last time I'd ever get between a woman and another man in my life. Who was it that said not to shoot the messenger? Shakespeare, most likely.

"You cannot say you saw him and then say you didn't. Either you did or you didn't."

"I didn't." I walked up to the front door of the farmhouse and stopped. "Goodbye, Pia."

The next day, my mum informed my father and me that the countess had invited us to join their family for dinner on the following Friday. I wanted nothing more than to beg off, and I would, feigning some sort of illness when the day arrived. I had no interest in seeing Pia…Well, I did, but I didn't want to argue with her or have her question me further about Paolo. I'd learned my lesson, and I'd not be butting in again. Besides, if they weren't broken up, he might be there, and that, I knew I couldn't stomach.

Turned out he was there, as was I. Pia acted as though nothing had happened between us, and while I wouldn't say she was openly demonstrative toward him, she didn't appear angry either.

Pia's father, though, was quite pleased her boyfriend was present, and less so that I was.

He and Paolo spoke in Italian most of the night, no matter how much scolding the countess gave them.

I didn't care. In fact, if neither said a word to me ever again, that would be perfectly okay by me.

I couldn't say the same for Pia. The longer the meal stretched on, along with the more wine she drank, the longer the daggers became she shot in her boyfriend's direction.

"Come with me," she said shortly after we finished eating the main course. She grabbed my hand and took off running through the vineyard, trailing me—the clambering elephant to Pia's gazelle—behind her.

When we came out of the other side of the long row of grapevines, the setting sun cast first the shorter wavelengths of violet and blue and, within what seemed like seconds, the longer ones of red, yellow, and orange upon the pool of water in front of us.

"Do you know how to swim?" she asked, slowly unbuttoning the tiny beads on the front of her dress.

"Of course I do, but…"

"But…what?"

"I don't have my togs."

"Togs?"

"Swim trunks."

"You English, so *prosaici.*"

I stepped closer and wrapped my hands around her wrists, stopping her from undressing further. I turned her in my arms so she faced away from me. "What's going on, Pia? Is your boyfriend ignoring you?"

She struggled, but I held on tight.

"What do you think will happen if he finds us swimming together? Will he pay attention then?"

"Non so di che cosa stai parlando."

"You know exactly what I'm talking about," I said, perhaps surprising her that I understood. I let her go, and she spun back around on me. Before she could speak, I grasped her arms. "Don't use me to make him jealous."

"Sei pazzo."

I let her go and walked away. Instead of going in the direction of the villa, I turned toward the farmhouse, leaving the beautiful, breathtaking Pia standing alone in the rays of the setting sun.

"Where did you run off to last night?" my mum asked the next morning when I came downstairs.

"I didn't feel well."

She raised a brow. "You and Pia left at the same time."

I loaded my plate with fruit and walked out to the *terrazza* where my father sat reading.

"Enjoying your time in Italy?" he asked, peering up at me with a smirk.

I shook my head and smiled, like him, noticing that Pia was headed our way.

2

With fists clenched, I stalked down the hillside to the farmhouse where Mylos was staying with his parents. Last night was the second time he'd walked away from me—*dismissed me*—and I was *furiosa*.

When my mamma told me an English family with a sixteen-year-old boy would be staying in the farmhouse for the summer, I never would've guessed Mylos was that boy.

He wasn't. He was a man. I watched him that first day when he waited while his mother got ripped off by the merchants at the market. Believe me, once they left, I gave them a piece of my Deltetto mind.

"We will not look favorably on your cheating our friends," I warned them. I hated *imbroglioni*—cheaters—which was why I'd reacted so badly when Mylos told me he saw Paolo in the village with "someone."

I'd longed suspected he saw other girls even though he swore he didn't. He said it was my own insecurity making me believe he'd cheat. That was true, at least in part.

We were children when we first met. My father and Paolo's were friends, and he came with his parents to visit. I was a skinny, awkward kid, and he was handsome enough to be a movie star.

When we were older and he came to visit again, I was stunned when he asked me to go on a date with him.

In my mind, I was still the awkward kid and he the movie star. There were times I still wondered why he was interested in sixteen-year-old me—especially since I wouldn't "put out" like he wanted me to.

But back to Mylos—he was always on my mind these days. In fact, Paolo and I had been arguing about him when he heard us shouting at each other. Paolo had caught me daydreaming, and when he asked if it was about the boy, I corrected him and said he was a man. *Stupida,* I know. He'd caught me off guard, and before Mylos was around, I was never off guard.

That day, when he stood with his back to me, his arms folded on the roof of the Fiat his parents had rented, I felt a longing unlike any I'd ever known. I got lost in the way his tight, firm ass looked in his shorts.

His legs were sinewy and muscular, and his back and shoulders were broad and chiseled.

When he turned around, I could see the outline of his taut abs through his t-shirt. Not to mention, I almost crossed myself when I lowered my eyes to the bulge between his legs. *Santa Madre di Dio.*

He didn't notice, though. I couldn't say whether I was relieved or disappointed. Instead, his smoldering, deep-set brown eyes looked me up and down like I was a sweet, innocent Italian *signorina* in my little flowered dress.

It wasn't like I was a *puttana,* but I wasn't completely innocent either. The temptation I felt that day, looking at the man-boy who smiled at me, was shameful. When I went to bed that night, I imagined that Mylos was the man who would finally take my virginity, and I would take his. I don't know how I knew he was still *innocente,* but I did. The idea of it fueled fantasies so intense, I nearly called out his name when my fingers brought me to release.

I could see him now on the *terrazza* with his father. He came out, set a plate on the table, and then watched me as I walked toward him. Even at only sixteen, he was taller than Paolo. The stubble covering his chin was dark like his hair and made him look older.

There was nothing about Mylos that screamed *ragazzo*. He was all sculpted, strapping, hard *uomo*.

"Good morning, Pia," he said with a smirk when I approached.

"*Buongiorno,* Mylos, *Signore* Stone." His father waved before standing, picking up his plate, and going inside.

"Would you like some fruit?" Mylos asked, motioning to his plate.

"*Sì.*" I reached over and took a handful of grapes. "*Grazie.*"

"Why are you here, Pia?"

"You were wrong last night."

He raised his eyebrows. "Was I?"

"Paolo and I…he doesn't own me."

Mylos pulled out a chair and motioned for me to sit. When I did, so did he.

"We are dating. That is all."

He bent his elbow on the table and rested his chin in his hand. "What you do, or don't do, is none of my business."

"You wouldn't swim with me last night."

"No. I wouldn't. Not like that."

"*Not like that.* What does that mean?"

He leaned forward and rested his elbows on his knees. He was close enough that I could reach out and touch his face.

"Tell me the truth, Pia. If your boyfriend hadn't been talking to your father all night, would you still have pulled me away from dinner to go swimming?"

I shrugged. "Maybe."

He sat back and laughed. "You're a liar."

I should be offended, but he was right. I was lying. When I didn't say anything, he leaned forward again. This time, he touched my arm with his fingertip.

"If you want to swim with me, then invite me, but not because you're trying to make another guy jealous. Do it because you want to spend time with me."

"Do you have a brother?"

His eyes scrunched. "No. Why?"

I shook my head and looked out over the vineyard. "It is impossible that you are sixteen."

He laughed, but it didn't bother me. Not like it did when Paolo laughed at me.

"Go swimming with me," I blurted.

"I'd like that. When?"

His gentle touch on my arm gave me chills. I shuddered and moved away from him. "Tonight, at sunset."

"No Paolo?"

"No."

He grabbed my hand before I could move farther away. It felt so good, so strong. I longed for him to pull me into his arms and kiss me. I wouldn't have cared who saw, even Paolo.

"Tell me what you're thinking."

My cheeks flushed; I could feel them. "Why?"

"Because I think I'd like whatever it is."

I shook my head, pulled my hand from his, and walked away.

"*Ci vediamo presto,* Mylos."

"*Quando il sole tramonta,* Pia."

"*Sì*, when the sun sets."

The rest of the afternoon passed slowly. I checked the time again and again while I worked in the winery office. It took almost a year after the first time I'd asked, for my father to allow me to help. It was only after I showed him how our computers could spit out reports in minutes, instead of the hours he spent poring through handwritten journals, that he finally consented.

Now, though, he expected the reports no later than noon each day and sometimes additional ones at closing time. I'd created a monster, but I loved every minute I spent working here, whether it was doing things like running reports or being in the winery itself, recording the readings on the fermentation tanks.

I pulled the papers from the printer and looked them over. Sales for the vintages we'd just released were strong; my father would be pleased. Perhaps it would soften him up enough that he wouldn't scold me for spending time with Mylos.

"What are you thinking about?"

"*Dio mio,* Georgio! You scared me."

"You're lost in thought."

I turned my chair to face him. Georgio and I had been friends since we were *ragazzi*. His mamma was our cook. Nonna Bella, as everyone called her, and Georgio lived in a *piccola casa* on the estate.

Lucia, the third in our band of makeshift musketeers, was the daughter of Elio and Carina Cesare. Her father was the head winemaker for Valentini, and her mother was our housekeeper. Her family didn't live on the estate, so she wasn't around as much as Georgio.

Since none of us had brothers or sisters, we'd become like siblings to one another.

I bent my elbow on the desk and rested my chin in my hand. "I'm going to break up with Paolo."

"Good. *È un lecchino*—always kissing up to your papà."

I shrugged. Georgio was right. However, my father was as much to blame.

Paolo's family owned an estate and winery in Chianti bigger than ours. While he was the second son and unable to inherit, my parents saw him as a good match for me. Something told me my papà had started planning our arranged union shortly after I was born.

I shuddered. I was far too young to be thinking of things like marriage—to anyone. Time to change the subject. "So, how are you, Georgio?"

"Hot. Bored."

"Me too." July in Tuscany could be miserable. August was worse, which was why millions of Italians took their holiday then.

"Let's sneak off to the beach. You, me, and Lucia."

I swatted his arm. "Sneak off? *Sei pazzo.*"

"Come on, you know you want to."

I laughed. "You have to work, and so do I."

Three years ago, Georgio had started working in the winery. This year, he was promoted to an apprentice to the head winemaker.

"We're too young to be working all the time."

I rolled my eyes. "Georgio, you were the one who wanted to work in the winery. Now you're saying you don't?"

"I'm saying we can take a couple of days off."

I shook my head and went back to compiling my father's reports.

"Anyway, I'm glad you're going to break up with Paolo. I never liked him."

I laughed. "You've never liked any of my boyfriends."

"I can't help it if I don't think anyone is good enough for you."

When the door opened and my papà walked in, Georgio immediately stood to leave. "See you later, Pia."

My father glared at him as he walked out. "He shouldn't be in here."

"Georgio is like family, Papà."

My father studied the reports I'd just finished preparing. "He's not family. He's the help," he grumbled.

I stood and kissed my papà's cheek. He meant well. I knew that. But if there was anyone my father didn't have to protect me from, it was Georgio.

I had just changed into my bikini and was ready to slip out and walk down to the pool to meet Mylos, when I saw my father talking to Georgio on the villa's *terrazza*.

I crept over to the sitting room and stood by the window where they couldn't see me. While they spoke in hushed voices, I could tell by my papà's tone that he was angry. I hoped he wasn't scolding Georgio for coming into the winery office to talk to me.

"Eavesdropping?" asked my mother, who walked in, carrying a book.

"Why is Papà so upset?"

She sighed. "Georgio pushes for modernization. Your father thinks he takes advantage of your friendship and speaks when he shouldn't. I have to agree that it isn't his place."

As much as I didn't want to, even I had to concede that he shouldn't be talking directly to my father. He should be speaking with Elio. He was the head winemaker and the man Georgio worked for.

"By the way, your father was on his way inside to talk to you. He wants you to go to Campania with him."

"When?"

She looked me up and down. "Tonight."

"Why do I have to go?"

Mamma sighed and took off her reading glasses, but chewed on the part that went over her ear. "Pia, your father needs you to go with him on winery business, and you will go. You're always telling him you want to run the winery someday. Prove it to him. Go get dressed and pack a bag for overnight. Maybe several days."

She put her glasses back on, stood, and walked out of the room. I looked outside and saw my father and Georgio were still arguing. It would be impossible for me to slip past them to tell Mylos I couldn't swim with him, but I had to get word to him somehow. If I tried, Papà would ask me where I was going, and that wasn't a conversation I wanted to have.

I went upstairs, changed out of my bikini, and packed a bag like my mamma told me to. I jotted a note to Mylos and then went looking for Lucia.

"I heard you have to go to Campania," she said when I found her in the kitchen.

I hung my head. *"Sì."*

"I wish I could go to Campania."

Between Lucia, Georgio, and me, she was the dreamer—filled with wanderlust. She talked about traveling places I'd never even heard of. I envied that about her. For me, I was most comfortable at home.

"Someday, you will be the one to go on sales trips."

"Georgio will make the wine, and you will run the winery."

"Sì," I said again, smiling at the plan we'd made back when we were little children. I pressed an envelope into her hand. "Please take this to Mylos for me. I was supposed to meet him at the pool at sunset."

Lucia wiggled her eyebrows. "I could go in your place."

"Don't get any ideas," I scolded.

"I thought you were with Paolo?"

Technically, I still was, but as soon as I got back from Campania, I intended to break up with him.

When my father and I returned several days later and drove past the farmhouse, it looked closed up, like it did when no one was staying in it. I studied my father, who didn't appear to notice.

When we got to the main house, my mamma ran out to greet us. After she hugged and kissed my father, she put her arm through mine.

"Did the family that was staying in the farmhouse leave?"

"Sì. C'è stata un'emergenza."

"What kind of emergency?"

"Pia! That's hardly our business."

I took my bag to my room, flopped on the bed, and covered my eyes with my arm. Could it really be that I'd never see Mylos again?

I heard the door creak open and feigned sleep, thinking it was my mother.

"He asked me to give this to you," Lucia whispered as she tucked something under my waist. I waited for the door to close before I opened my eyes and grabbed the envelope.

Dear Pia,

I'm sorry I didn't get the chance to say goodbye. My mother's sister passed away suddenly, and we were forced to cut our holiday short. I hope to return to Italy one day soon.

Yours truly,
"Mylos"

I folded the note and put it back in the envelope. I was disappointed. More than that. What I felt was profound, as though the universe had put us in one another's paths, and instead of following the course laid out for us, we'd each gone our separate ways. Somewhere, a guardian angel was fighting back tears just like I was.

3

Grinder
Two Years Later
London, England

"Have you heard back from her?" my sister asked.

"Not yet."

"What will you do?"

"I haven't decided."

For the past two years, I'd thought a lot about Pia. Fourteen days after our family's abrupt departure from Italy, I'd received a letter from her in answer to my note. In it, she told me how disappointed she was that we didn't have the chance to get to know one another better and she hoped that, one day soon, we'd be able to swim together at sunset.

Included in the envelope was a heart-shaped, multifaceted stone to remember her by. I'd taken that letter—but not the stone—to Lily and asked her whether she thought Pia was being flirtatious. She'd rolled her eyes and smacked me. "You really can't be that daft, Miles. Of course she is."

I'd written back, and so had Pia. About once a week, I'd receive a letter from her and would immediately answer. The last one I wrote, though, went unanswered. It had been three weeks, and I was trying my hardest not to read anything into it. My sister asking me daily if I'd received anything wasn't helping.

In less than a month, I'd be graduating from secondary school. A few weeks later, I'd begin training at the Royal Military Academy Sandhurst—known to most simply as Sandhurst. My plan was to become an officer in the British Army. The two-year training program would be rigorous, and at the end, I would join the ranks in service to my country.

My mum wasn't pleased when I announced my acceptance, but my father had enthusiastically given his consent.

In my unreciprocated correspondence, I'd told Pia I hoped to come to Italy before I had to report to the academy. I wouldn't have much time, but at least we'd be able to see each other again.

That she hadn't responded, stung. Perhaps I made too much of what she'd written to me. What to me was a longing to see her again, to her may have been a flirtation she hadn't expected me to act on.

Feeling foolish, I pulled the heart-shaped stone she'd sent me out of my pocket and studied it. Since the day it arrived, I'd carried it with me everywhere. It had become my touchstone. Perhaps it was time to let go of the foolish boyhood crush it represented. I set it on my dresser and walked out of the room. Before I was all the way downstairs, though, I raced up and put it back in my pocket. Silly or not, I felt a certain sense of peace when I carried it with me.

The day after my graduation, my parents were leaving on their annual summer holiday, this time to the Algarve region of Portugal. I'd begged off going for even a week, saying I had to prepare for my departure to Sandhurst.

"We'll be off, then," said my mother, reaching up to kiss my cheek. "Won't you change your mind and join us?"

I shook my head. "Thank you, but no. Too much to do and all that."

"Right," she said, her eyes scrunching as she handed me an envelope.

"What's this?"

"Our gift to you, Miles," said my father as I pulled out the round-trip ticket to Florence. "It seems you might have some unfinished business in Tuscany."

I looked over his shoulder at my sister, who couldn't contain her smile. Once our mum and dad were off, she'd be getting an earful from me. She'd obviously orchestrated this "gift."

"You'd best pack, Miles," said my mother. "Your flight leaves at the same time ours does."

"Seriously?" I looked at the ticket a second time. Yes, it was for today. "Bollocks," I muttered, rushing up the stairs to grab my things.

As I made my way back down, I reached into my pocket and pulled out the red stone, hoping the girl who'd given it to me would be happy to see me.

I cheek-kissed my parents when we arrived at the airport and then rushed over to the agent, thrusting my ticket at him.

"Your first visit to Italy?" he asked as he stamped my passport.

"Second," I answered.

"*Buon viaggio!*"

I hurried through security and got to the gate just as they announced early boarding.

By the time the plane landed in Florence, I was back to feeling trepidatious. Rather than hiring a car to go to Val d'Orcia tonight, I decided to spend a few days in Florence. It was something I'd wanted to do on our visit two years ago, but once I'd met Pia, I forgot about anything in Italy other than her.

As I passed by the counters where travelers could hire cars, I felt pulled to rent one. If I were spending the next few days in Florence, having a vehicle would prove more of a nuisance. In fact, it would be impossible, given cars weren't allowed in the ancient city, except those who held special permits.

Telling myself I'd spend time in Florence after I saw Pia, I succumbed, knowing full well I'd spend the ninety-minute drive lamenting my decision.

Driving through the gates of *Antica Cascina dei Conti di Valentini,* memories of my time here came rushing back to me. I was struck that it was even more beautiful than I remembered.

I drove up to the farmhouse, relieved it didn't appear as though anyone had rented it. Just for the heck of it, I got out and walked up to the front door. When I knocked, it unlatched and slowly opened.

"Hello?" I called out, but no one answered. I walked into the kitchen, calling out again, but found it empty. Feeling assured I wasn't intruding on someone's holiday, I ran up the stairs to the room that had been mine.

It was as though time had stood still. Everything looked exactly the same. I flopped on the bed and clasped my hands under my head. I closed my eyes and thought back to when I first saw Pia. If only her laughter would drift up to me now. I'd look out as I did that day, and she would see me. We would race to each other, and I'd lift her in my arms, twirling her in a circle before I covered her lips with mine and kissed her.

I bolted upright when I heard the front door open and close. Jumping up, I made my way to the top of the staircase. "Hello?" I called out.

"Tu chi sei?" asked a man standing just inside the front door. I recognized him. *Paolo*—the guy she told me she broke up with.

"Sorry, I stayed here a couple of years ago and got caught in reminiscing. If you've let the place, I apologize for my intrusion." When I got to the bottom of the stairs, feigning ignorance to a possible relationship between him and Pia, I stuck my hand out to shake his. He didn't do the same.

"You're trespassing," he responded, scowling.

"Right. Like I said, my apologies. I'm actually here to see Pia."

The man's hooded eyes went almost black, and he folded his arms. "She isn't here."

"I can see that, but is she at home?" I motioned in the direction of the villa.

"No."

"I've traveled from England and was hoping to see her before I have to return. Will she be back later today?"

"No," he repeated.

"Tomorrow, then?"

When he shook his head, I ran my hand through my hair. "Very well. I'll just find a place in town and try to reach her."

"Pia doesn't want to see you."

"Look, mister…I didn't catch your last name."

"Viticcio."

"Right. Viticcio. Pia and I are friends. I'm sure if she knew I was here, she'd be happy to see me."

Before I realized what was happening, the man had me by the shirt collar and pushed me out the front door.

"She isn't here, and if she were, she wouldn't want to see you. As I said before, you're trespassing." He let me go with a shove.

As tempted as I was, I didn't put my hands on him. In a few days' time, I was due to report to the Royal Military Academy. The last thing I needed was an incident in a foreign country. "The Pia I know makes decisions for herself."

The man grinned, but not at all in a friendly way. "Not anymore."

"What does that mean?"

"I'm her fiancé, and I make the decisions as to whom she sees and doesn't see."

I wondered if that was truly the case. If so, Pia was a very different person than the one I'd met two years ago.

I got in the car and pounded my fist on the steering wheel as I drove out the gates of the estate, wondering how I could've been so bloody stupid. *Pia hadn't answered me.* Shouldn't that have been enough for me to realize she didn't want to see me?

Instead of driving back to Florence, I went in the opposite direction. I had no idea where I was headed, but I hoped it was somewhere I could forget all about Pia Deltetto.

4

Pia

I bit my bottom lip and took another step toward the front door. I'd been standing in front of the address on the letters I received from Mylos for twenty minutes, trying to talk myself into knocking on the door.

This truly had to be the craziest thing I ever did. A week ago, when I decided to travel to London on my own, not knowing if Mylos would be home, and if he was, whether he'd want to see me, it had seemed *romantic* and *adventurous*. Now it seemed stupid and expensive, given I'd soon be taking a taxi back to the airport to exchange my ticket and return to Italy if I couldn't muster the courage to just knock on the damn door.

I hadn't made a move in either direction when the front door opened and a woman walked toward me.

"May I help you?" she asked, eyeing the envelope in my hand. Before I could answer, she gasped. *"Are you Pia?"*

I bit my bottom lip again. *"Sì."*

"Come in, for goodness' sake," she said, pulling me with her. "I'm Lily, by the way, Miles' sister."

I stopped when we got to the door. "I don't want to intrude."

She rolled her eyes, but she was still smiling. "God, you sound just like him."

She led me inside, took my bag from my hand, and set it on the floor. "Can I get you a cup of tea?"

"Um, sure. Thank you." I looked around the small kitchen that reminded me of Mylos' mother. There were teapots and cups, plates, and towels, all with different floral patterns. If I closed my eyes, I could see her in this space, puttering around, talking to herself all the while. I loved my mamma, but Mylos' mother made my heart happy.

I looked up at Lily, who was studying me. "I know why Miles likes you so much."

"You do?" I didn't.

"Everything you're thinking is written on your face."

"Oh, yeah?" I put one hand on my hip. "What was I thinking just now?"

"What a quaint kitchen this is, and how fascinating you find it to be."

I had to give it to her. "Close."

"What did I miss?"

"I can see your mother in this kitchen. It looks like her."

"See? And while another person might think that would be insulting, because of the look on your face, it's endearing."

It seemed like a stupid question, but I asked anyway. "Is Mylos home?"

She shook her head. "He isn't, and you won't believe it when I tell you where he is." She set a plate of cookies in front of me and then poured the tea. "Cream or sugar?"

"Yes, both, please."

"So," she said, taking a seat. "My brother is in Italy. To visit you, by the way."

"*Santa Madre di Dio.* Are you serious?" I put my head in my hand. "But why didn't he tell me? Why didn't he write?"

Lily cocked her head. "He did."

"When?"

"Weeks ago. You didn't respond."

I pulled the letter out of my pocket. "This was the last I received from him."

She studied the postmark. "He wrote another after this one."

"I didn't get it."

"Right. Well, this is a bloody mess."

I scooted my chair back; Lily put her hand on my arm.

"You can't be thinking of leaving."

"He isn't here. I'm…intruding." I knew I'd said it before, but I couldn't think of a better word.

"Before you go anywhere, let me try to reach him."

She left the room and came back a few minutes later with a cell phone. "Straight to voicemail."

"Okay." This time when I stood, she put her hand on my shoulder.

"Where are you staying?"

"I'm not."

Lily shook her head. "You aren't going anywhere until I reach my brother. Your luck, your airplanes will pass in the air." She tapped her cheek with her finger, something I often did too. "Look, my parents are in Portugal, and I'm here on my own. Stay with me until we can sort this mess out."

"I don't want to—"

"Intrude? You're not. Worst-case scenario, I'll show you around London, unless you've been here before."

"I haven't."

"Come on." She motioned for me to follow and picked up my bag. "You can stay in Miles' room." When she winked and nudged me, I smiled.

I opened my lids the next morning, shielding my eyes from the sun that poured in through the window. My head was pounding, and I felt like I'd eaten a cotton ball.

When we didn't hear back from Mylos, Lily convinced me to go with her to meet some friends at a pub not far from the house.

I couldn't remember when I'd last had so much fun. Lily's boyfriend, William, and several other people joined us, telling stories about Mylos for much of the night. The one we laughed about the most, though, was the fact he'd gone to Italy in search of me, and here I was in London.

"It's so romantic," said one of the girls, whose name I couldn't remember now. I could remember the look on her face, though. It had been wistful in a way that made my heart hurt. Sure, it was a great story, but not while I was living it. I hoped he'd call today. If he didn't, I should probably accept it as not meant to be and go home.

The next three days, I woke up with the same resolution, and Lily talked me out of it. She kept her promise of showing me around London. Each day was more fun than the one before. Tomorrow, though, I had to leave no matter what.

There was still no word from Mylos. Lily had given up leaving messages, saying instead that she was the one who'd lucked out and had a new best friend. "He never checks his bloody mobile anyway," she muttered over our morning cup of tea. "I'm sorry, Pia. I truly am."

We both jumped out of our seats when we heard the front door opening.

"*Miles!*" shouted Lily, racing out of the kitchen. "Where in the hell have you been?"

He rounded the corner, and his mouth dropped open. "Pia? What are you doing here?"

Lily smacked him. "She's here to see you, you tosser."

"But…"

"She didn't get your letter, so she came looking for you."

Mylos glared at his sister. "Would you mind letting Pia speak for herself?"

"Sure, of course," she said, shrugging and smiling. "I'll just be in my room." She silently clapped her hands and jumped up and down behind his back before she ran up the stairs.

Once she was gone, Mylos scrubbed his face with his hand. "Explain this to me once more."

I bit my lip, wishing he seemed happier to see me. "Like Lily said, I didn't get the last letter you sent. I wrote again, but when that went unanswered, I decided to come here. It was probably stupid, but…I had to see you again, Mylos." When I took a step closer to him, he stepped back. Why was he acting this way? "I don't understand. She said you went to Italy to see me."

He pulled a chair out from the table, but didn't sit in it. Instead, he put his hands on the back of it, almost like it was a barrier between us.

"I did, Pia, but when your fiancé was the first person I ran into, I saw the error of my ways."

"My *what*?"

"Your fiancé. You know, the man you're going to marry."

"I don't know who you talked to, but you must've misunderstood. I don't have a fiancé, and I'm definitely not getting married." I held out my hands as though showing him I had no ring would prove I wasn't lying.

"Paolo—the guy you told me you broke up with."

"Paolo?"

"That's right. When he found me at the farmhouse, he told me I was trespassing."

"This is crazy. I'm not engaged, Mylos. Not to Paolo or anyone else. If I were, I wouldn't have traveled to England to see you."

"Then, why did he say you were? Why was he even there?"

"I don't know, and believe me, I intend to find out." While I knew my father had hired Paolo to help at the winery, it made no sense that he would tell Mylos we were engaged.

When Mylos didn't make any kind of move, I realized he still thought I was lying.

"I'm sorry I came." When I turned to walk out, I saw Lily in the hallway around the corner.

"Uh-uh. No way. You aren't going anywhere." She pulled me back into the kitchen and stood in front of her brother. "This woman came all the way to London to see you. *To see you!*" She smacked the side of his head. "You're a bloody idiot if you think she'd lie to you, and if you do, then you aren't my brother."

When he didn't say anything, Lily made a sound of disgust and grabbed my arm again. "Come on, Pia. You don't need this crap."

"Pia, Lily, wait…"

My eyes filled with tears, and I couldn't turn around and look at him.

"Lily, give us a moment."

"Do you want me to?" she asked.

I nodded.

"Fix this, Miles," she said and ran back upstairs.

Seconds later, I felt his hands on my shoulders. "Forgive me. I've spent the last few days roaming around Italy, trying to mend a very foolish, broken heart and drinking away my self-pity."

I took a deep breath and slowly turned around to face him. "How can you say you have a broken heart and then call me a liar?"

He put his hands back on my shoulders and leaned down to look into my eyes. "I'm sorry," he repeated. "I just assumed that was the reason you never answered me."

"Do you still think I am engaged even though I've told you repeatedly that I'm not?"

He shook his head.

"What made you change your mind?"

"I guess Lily smacking me jarred my brain back into gear." He squeezed my shoulders. "Forgive me?"

I folded my arms. "I wouldn't lie to you, Mylos, and I'm not an…*imbrogliona*—a cheater."

"I'm an idiot. One who's begging you to forgive me."

His warm brown eyes were pleading as much as his words.

"On one condition."

"Name it."

"Kiss me."

Mylos took a step forward, put his hand on the back of my neck, and captured my mouth with his.

Oh, how I'd longed to know how it would feel to be kissed by him. His soft lips became hard. His tongue circled mine, and we devoured each other's mouths.

"Pia," he groaned, weaving his fingers in my hair before taking my mouth again. I put my hands on his chest, dug my fingers into the chiseled muscles, and let my body melt into his.

"Wait." Somehow, I found the strength to pull away from him. Instead of letting me, he jerked my body into his and brought his lips back to my mouth.

"Do you know how long I've wanted to do that?" he asked before capturing my tongue with his. He held my face with his hand and pressed harder. "I don't want to stop, Pia."

"Get a room," we both heard Lily say as she laughed and walked out the front door. Before she closed it, she stuck her head back in. "In fact, there's one right at the top of the stairs. Have fun, kids."

The door closed behind her, but her interruption had been enough to make both of us lean back.

Mylos ran his hand through his hair and took a deep breath. "Tell me again why you're here."

My mind was reeling with want. Why had I come to England? "I wanted to see you again, Mylos."

"Come with me," he said, pulling me to the front door. "I can't be alone with you and not touch you." He held my hand and led me outside. "I'm starving. Have you eaten?"

It took a minute for his words to register. Had I? I couldn't remember. I shook my head. "No. I don't think so."

He laughed and leaned down to kiss me. It was a quick brush of his lips on mine, and then he kept walking.

"You're taller," I murmured, realizing that my head no longer reached his shoulder.

"Yeah? Well, you're just as sexy as you've always been." He nuzzled my neck, and my knees went weak.

"Mylos," I groaned.

"Right. Food."

No—that wasn't what I meant at all.

When we got to the pub where Lily had taken me my first night in London, Mylos found a table and then sat across from me. After the barmaid took our order, he leaned forward and rested his forearms on the surface. "Hi, Pia."

I smiled. "Hi, Mylos."

"Have I told you how much I love the way you say my name?"

I felt my cheeks flush, and I looked down. He reached over and put his hand on mine.

"I'm so glad you're here."

"Me too."

"How long are you?"

I sighed. "I'm leaving in the morning."

"Tomorrow?"

I nodded.

"Can't you stay a while longer? I mean, a couple of days?"

"I can't." I barely had time to get home and pack before I needed to leave for Siena. While it wasn't far, I was living on campus and had to check into the dorms before my classes started.

"Right. It was unfair of me to ask."

"What about you? Aren't you starting your training soon?"

"I report in three days." He ran one hand through his hair. "God, I bloody hate that we wasted so much time." He squeezed my hand. "So, you didn't say why exactly you have to get back."

"I'm starting at the university."

"What? That's brilliant."

I smiled. It was something I'd admitted to him in one of my letters. It wasn't expected that I'd go to college, but I really wanted to. If it weren't for Mylos convincing me I should, I might not have been brave enough to bring it up to my father. As it was, it had taken some persuasion on my part, particularly when I told him I wanted to study business so I could run the winery someday.

"I'm really happy for you, Pia."

"If it weren't for you..."

"Nah, you would've done it anyway. How did the conversation go with your father, by the way?"

I laughed. "He thought I was *pazza*—crazy. But he finally gave in. My mamma helped talk him into letting me go. I'm sure there's a part of him that hopes I'll drop out and get married." I laughed. "But not to Paolo." Actually, if I did, it would make my father very happy, but I wouldn't tell Mylos that.

"I'm so proud of you." He smiled, and it was so beautiful, it made my heart hurt.

"I'm proud of you too."

We talked more as we shared each other's food. Unlike the other time I'd been at this pub, I stopped drinking after one pint. When I told him about spending an evening here with Lily and her friends, he laughed.

"I should've known you'd get on well."

"I was going to leave, that first day, but she convinced me to stay."

"Thank God," he murmured, stroking the back of my hand with his thumb. "I want to kiss you again."

"I'd like that."

He paid the tab, and we left the pub, stopping to kiss every so often on the way to his house. When we walked up to the front door, he put his hand on the side of my face. "I want to be with you, Pia. But if it isn't something you want…"

"I do, Mylos."

We laughed as he fumbled with his keys. "I'm a little nervous."

"Me too."

He was about to stick the key in the lock when the door opened.

"Miles!" exclaimed his father. "And Pia! What are you both doing here?"

"I'm sorry about this," Mylos whispered to me after he explained what had happened to his parents and how we both ended up in London.

"I'm just happy to be with you," I whispered back.

His arm around my shoulders made me feel safe, protected, like I could always rely on him. When he told me the reason he wanted to join the military was to protect the innocent from harm, I knew it was the exact right thing for him.

"So," said his mother after we finished dinner. "Sleeping arrangements?"

"Mum," groaned Mylos, and his father laughed.

"Let them be, Margaret."

"Pia can stay where she is, in my room. I'll take the sofa," Mylos offered.

I saw his mother and father make eye contact. Even if they hadn't said a word about where we would sleep, I would've felt uncomfortable sleeping with Mylos in his boyhood home with his parents in the room next door. When—if—we ever made love, I wouldn't want it to feel like we were sneaking or doing something we shouldn't be.

"Feel like going for a walk?"

"I'd like that."

Instead of making love, Mylos and I walked around London, talking, laughing, and kissing until the sun came up.

We returned to his house with just enough time to grab my bag and get to the airport.

"These were the best twenty-four hours of my life," he said when he walked with me as far as airport security would allow.

"Mine too."

We kissed again and then again after that.

"I don't know whether I'll be able to get leave while I'm at Sandhurst, but I'll write, Pia."

"I'll write too, Mylos." I kissed him once more and then took a step back. "I have to go."

"I know."

"Goodbye, Mylos."

"*Arrivederci,* Pia."

5

Grinder
Two Years Later
Sandhurst, England

Being at Sandhurst was the worst and best two years of my life. It was quite hard to be away from my family, and I found there was little room for personal expression, in other words, having a personality. In my time at the academy, I experienced sleep deprivation, punishments for minor infringements, freezing-cold exercises, injuries, exhaustion, and a very steep learning curve. Nothing I experienced hurt or was harder than missing Pia, though.

Conversely, as a military officer to be, I thrived. Whenever there was a competition, which was daily or several times a day, I consistently landed in first or second place. The man who bested me at least half the time, became my best friend.

Keon Edgemon and I met during in-processing, and our rooms were next to each other. He was a good bloke—funny, intelligent, committed, and seemed to have an innate sense as to when I needed time on my own. It wasn't a trait many of our fellow cadets shared. Too often, I'd find myself in conversations I cared little of. More, I resented them. While the physical aspect of our training was rigorous, it was the academics that gave me the most pause. Keon, an ace student, would frequently rescue me by engaging offenders in his own conversation.

Our final day at the institution that had been around since 1802 and graduated innumerable officers into the British Army, culminated with a celebratory dinner, during which we'd be commissioned as second lieutenants and receive our first assignments. We'd also be given our call signs, initially put into place to save our true identities from the enemy when transmissions were intercepted. Now, it was more a rite of passage.

"I'm not much of a speechmaker," said our commander after we were officially commissioned, "so I'm going to get down to business. Each of you has a sealed envelope in front of you. You may open them now."

The sound of them being ripped open filled the hall; otherwise, it was silent.

"What did you get?" asked Keon, leaning close to me.

"Monckton."

"Brilliant."

"You too?"

"Affirmative."

Both Keon and I would be leaving Sandhurst and report directly to Fort Monckton, where we'd train for six months in the Intelligence Officer's New Entry Course. Only two cadets from each graduating class were selected for the program. Both Keon and I had applied, and as he said, it was brilliant that we were the ones chosen.

"Call sign?" I asked.

He rolled his eyes and handed me the piece of paper.

"Edge?"

"Also bloody brilliant," he deadpanned. "What's yours?"

"Grinder."

"Better than Stoner, I suppose."

I laughed. The call sign committee had not exercised much creativity in our assigned names. Those also seated at our table appeared to feel the same degree of disappointment.

I didn't care. Being accepted at Monckton was reward enough for the hard work I'd put in.

"Fancy a pint?" Keon asked after we'd collected our belongings and finished with our final room inspection.

"I could stand one."

"Ready to head back to London?" he asked as we sat at the local pub, celebrating our assignments.

"For now." We had seven days' leave before we had to report to Monckton. I'd given little thought to what I'd do other than catch up on a year's worth of missed sleep. That, and figuring out a way to see Pia.

So far, neither of us had been able to come up with a way to make it work. She was in the midst of final exams, and by the time they ended, I'd have to report for SIS training.

"You?"

"Traveling," he answered.

"Where to?"

"Somewhere in the Mediterranean."

"I envy you." I'd thought about going to Italy anyway and surprising Pia, but after the disastrous way that turned out the last time, I decided against it.

I'd been at Fort Monckton for three weeks when I finally received a letter back from Pia. While she didn't elaborate, she told me there were problems at Valentini and she wasn't certain she'd be able to continue attending university.

I sneaked off and rang her number a couple of times, but wasn't successful in reaching her. Not knowing when I'd have access to my mobile again, I left a message, saying I'd try again as soon as I could.

"Is everything okay?" Edge asked when I rejoined him in the dining hall.

"I fear not." I couldn't explain why, but I had a feeling there was something very wrong in Tuscany. I reached into my pocket and touched Pia's heart-shaped stone, praying I wasn't right.

***

Six months sped by, and before I knew it, Edge and I were getting ready to graduate from SIS training. While we didn't have our initial assignments yet, we were informed we'd have a minimum of fourteen days' leave before we'd have to report to wherever the British Army chose to send us.

"Gentlemen, a word," said our commanding officer as we were headed to pack up and check out. He led us into a conference room and closed the door.

"I'm sorry to do this now, but I have your orders."

I looked at Edge, who had the same worried expression I did.

"There's a situation in Central Iraq, in the city of Najaf. We've received intelligence indicating that certain members of the Iraqi military, supposedly our allies, have been systematically taking out coalition service members. Given your ages and recent military training, sending you both in on this mission makes a great deal of sense."

"What is the mission exactly?" asked Edge.

"It'll be your job to find and eliminate them."

I hated asking, but I had to know. "When do we report?"

He scrubbed his face with his hand. "You ship out to Baghdad in five days. Again, I'm sorry about the timing of this."

Once dismissed, I raced out of the main office and to my room. I'd told Edge he could ride back to London with my dad and me, but I was in no mood to wait. Somehow, I had to see Pia. *Had to.* I didn't care if it was only for a few hours.

"Listen, I know we talked about riding back to London together," I began when Edge walked in and sat on the bed.

He held up his hand. "Do what you need to do, Grind. I'll get a lift back with one of the other guys."

"Sorry, mate."

"Don't be. I'll see you in five days."

I rang Pia, hoping against all odds she'd answer, and she did.

"I'm sorry to be abrupt, but where are you?"

"I'm at Valentini. How are you, Mylos?"

"I'm deploying on a secret mission in five days." I heard her gasp. "Sweetheart, I need you to tell me whether or not I should come to Italy."

"Can you? Do you have time?"

"I can be on the next flight out to Florence."

"I'll be at the airport, waiting."

"Pia…"

"Whatever it is, say it, Mylos."

"I need you."

"I need you, too."

Four hours later, I raced out of customs at the Florence airport and into Pia's waiting arms. My heart raced as I touched her warm, open lips with my tongue, and the rest of the world went silent. There were no more birds singing, no sounds of the traffic that surrounded us. Even the wind stilled as I focused solely on the way her body shuddered as I brushed soft kisses from her mouth, down her neck, to the smattering of freckles on her bare shoulder.

"Tell me there's somewhere we can be alone."

"*Sì,*" she said, leading me outside to where a car sat waiting. "Do you want to know where we're going?"

I shook my head. "I don't care."

When the driver opened the back door and we got in, I pulled her into my arms and devoured her mouth like a starving man. We spent the next hour with our lips fused together in one long kiss.

The driver pulled up to what looked like a resort. I got out and waited for Pia to put her hand in mine. I pulled her close and kissed her again. "I can't get enough of you."

"Come," she said as I grabbed our bags from the driver and followed her down a walkway to a villa that looked like a miniature of the one at Valentini.

Once inside, she put her hands on the hem of my shirt; I grabbed the back and pulled it over my head.

"*Santa Madre di Dio.*" She rested her hand on my bare torso, leaned up, and kissed me.

"Pia," I breathed. "If you want me to stop…tell me now."

She wound her fingers in my hair and pulled me closer. My blood throbbed, and my heart beat frantically in my chest. All at once, I felt like we were melting into each other, our two bodies dissolving into one.

She reached up and slid her dress off her shoulders. It floated to the wood floor, landing in a heap at our feet and leaving her naked but for her pale-pink knickers.

"Touch me," she demanded, bringing my hand to her breast. I couldn't resist a taste. My mouth covered her nipple, and we both groaned. Her skin tasted like the sweetest honey; I wanted to lick her everywhere.

My lips trailed from her breast down the soft swell of her stomach. I lowered myself to my knees and pulled her body close to mine, breathing in her arousal. I gripped the fabric that was a thin barrier between my mouth and her sex and pulled it down her legs.

She took a step back, leaving them on the floor near her dress and held her hand out to me. I followed her up the stairs to the second level, my eyes glued to her arse and the way it moved, showing me just a glimpse between her legs before closing again. I put my hands on her hips, needing to touch her somewhere. When she stopped halfway up, I leaned forward and kissed her sweet arse cheek before sinking my teeth into her flesh.

She giggled and picked up her pace, running the rest of the way to the second floor. I chased after her. When she reached the bed, her playfulness dissolved into breathlessness.

"Wait," she said, climbing onto the bed and resting against the pillows. "Let me see you."

"My God, Pia," I groaned when she spread her legs and rested her hand on the glistening hair between them.

"Show me. Let me see you, Mylos." Her body writhed as I unfastened my zipper and lowered it, letting my shorts fall, and as I did, my cock sprang forth. Pia gasped and held her hand out to me.

"Let me touch you."

I knew that if she did, the first orgasm she and I shared would be by her touch. I wanted more than that, for both of us.

Instead, I knelt between her legs and ran my fingertips from the back of her knees up the inside of her thighs. I splayed my fingers, spreading her wider, opening her more. "I need to see you first."

I shifted so I was on my stomach, moving so close I could almost touch her with my tongue. Instead, I studied her pink flesh. Unable to resist, I kissed her.

Her fingers were back in my hair, pulling now instead of just gripping. "Mylos, please," she whined.

I ran one finger from the top of her wetness, through her folds, and sunk it into her warmth. My eyes rolled back in my head, and I moaned, thinking of how my cock would feel when it was in the same place my finger was.

I added a second finger, slowly moving it in and out, but not deep. She felt so tight I feared I'd hurt her. I leaned forward again and kissed her, this time running my tongue where my fingers had traveled.

Pia's hips bucked from the bed, and she cried out for me to do it again. When I did, she suddenly stopped moving. I watched in utter fascination as she fell apart in my arms, crying out my name as she came. As quickly as she'd stilled, she reached out and took my cock in her hand. I covered hers with mine. "Not yet, my beautiful Pia. I need to be inside you."

"Mylos." I looked up at her. "Did you bring something? *Preservativo?*"

"A condom?"

"*Sí.*"

I lifted myself from her, stood, and walked over to where my bag sat on the floor. I reached inside and pulled out a foil packet. I ripped it open with my teeth and sheathed myself.

"Next time, I want to do that."

I had to grab myself to keep from coming. "You're killing me, you know that?"

She held her hand out to me, and I got back on the bed and settled my body between her still-spread legs. "I've wanted you like this for so long. Pia, I…"

"Shh." She put her fingertips on my lips. "This is right, Mylos. You and I were meant to do this."

I entered her slowly, gently, keeping my eyes glued to hers.

"More."

I pushed a little farther in until I felt like I couldn't go any deeper. Pia reached around and put her hands on the cheeks of my arse. "Now, Mylos," she said before she pulled me against her at the same time she thrust her body toward mine. When she cried out, I wanted to stop, but she wouldn't let me.

Our bodies took on a rhythm I had as little control over as I did the release I knew was only moments away. I stilled and our eyes met.

"Now, Mylos."

As I began to move again, her fingernails dug into my flesh. My jaw flexed and I thrust once, twice, and with the third, she cried out in the same way she had when I touched her with my tongue.

I would never forget the look on her face or the way her eyes bored into mine. There were no truer words spoken than what she'd said only a few minutes ago. She and I were meant to do this. No one else, nothing, could be as perfect as this was.

With my gaze affixed to hers, I began to thrust again. Pia rocked her body against mine, and I came apart just like she had.

6

Pia

Mylos and I had three beautiful days together before I had to take him back to the airport. I tried not to cry as he was leaving, but I couldn't stop myself.

"Shh…" he murmured. "I'll be back as soon as I can."

I nodded through my tears, praying harder than I ever had for God to keep him safe.

I watched him walk away and lingered even after I couldn't see him anymore. Finally, after I knew his plane had taken off, I walked out of the airport and over to the parking structure where I'd left my car when he first arrived, knowing I wouldn't be able to keep my mind on driving.

Before I pulled out of the space, my cell rang. I looked at the screen and saw it was someone calling from a Valentini phone number.

"*Sì?*"

"Pia, there's been an accident. We need you to come home." Georgio's voice sounded strained to the point of breaking.

"What's happened, Georgio?"

"It's your father."

I crossed myself. "*Santa Madre di Dio.*"

"He's very badly injured."

"Where is he?"

"Ospedale Di Montepulciano."

"I'll be there as quickly as I can be."

In the last couple of years, so much had gone wrong at Valentini, I couldn't help but wonder if God was punishing our family. For what, I didn't know.

I rushed into the hospital; Georgio was just inside the entrance.

"This way," he said, leading me to the elevator.

He didn't speak and I asked no questions. Until I saw my father, I wouldn't be able to think straight.

"Papà!" I rushed over to his bedside after Georgio escorted me to the room. Both of his legs were in casts and elevated. *"Dio santo!"* I shook my head as tears ran down my cheeks.

"Pia, *bellissima,* I told Georgio not to bother you with this."

"Bother me? You've been seriously injured, Papà."

The door opened and my mamma came in. When I rushed over and put my arms around her, she put her head on my shoulder and cried.

I heard my father groan. "It's a couple of broken legs."

I had to cover my mouth when I saw the look my mother gave him. If looks could kill, broken legs would be the least of his worries.

"What happened, Papà? Do you feel up to talking about it?"

"No. I am very tired, Pia. Perhaps tomorrow." My father's eyes weren't on me as he spoke; he was looking at Georgio.

"Are you sure you'll be okay? I can stay overnight."

My father patted my cheek. "Take your mamma home, Pia. Make sure she rests."

"We'll be back in the morning."

"*Sì.*" He nodded, his eyes drifting closed, perhaps because of the painkillers.

Georgio followed us to the elevators. "Did you see what happened?" I asked while we waited.

He shook his head but looked in my mother's direction.

As I drove my mamma to the house, my mind raced with the other things that had gone wrong at Valentini since I first left for college.

Within weeks of me moving into the dorms in Siena, there was a malfunction in the room that held the stainless tanks used to ferment the white wines. We lost an entire year's worth of juice when the cooling system went down for an indeterminate amount of time. That was the part that bothered me the most. People were in and out of the wine rooms all the time. How could it be that no one noticed? Perhaps if they had, we could have corrected the problem before the juice went bad.

Then there was an accident involving our head winemaker when the ventilation system in one of the fermentation rooms stopped working, much in the same way the cooling system had. Given the amount of carbon dioxide released during fermentation, adequate ventilation was essential to guard against the risk of CO2 poisoning.

Fortunately, one of the workers had gone looking for him and found him passed out. If he hadn't gotten the man outside when he did, he might've died. Still, he'd been hospitalized for several weeks. After he was released, he'd informed my father he was still too weak to return to work.

The third and final emergency, before my father's accident, involved a break-in where several thousand dollars' worth of wine were stolen. As with the other equipment malfunctions, the security system had failed, allowing the thieves access to the storage rooms and leaving us with no video surveillance to determine who they were.

"Pia, what is on your mind?" asked my mamma, who I thought had fallen asleep.

"I'm worried about Papà."

"*Sì*. As am I."

"Do you know what happened, Mamma?"

She nodded with hooded eyes. "He was run over by a forklift."

My head snapped in her direction. *"What? Are you serious?"* I looked back at the road, gripping the steering wheel so tightly my knuckles were white. "He could have died."

"But he didn't."

"How can you be so calm? So many things have gone wrong at Valentini."

She shrugged. "It's the nature of the business. There are accidents. Things are stolen. The difference is, these things seem to have happened all at once."

"You aren't suspicious about Papà's accident?" I was incredulous. Had someone given her a sedative?

"I didn't say that."

"Explain what you meant, then."

"I'm suspicious of all of it, my dear daughter. As I said, it's the nature of the business that someone would want to drive us out of it."

The next day, when my mamma and I went to the hospital, the doctors told us the prognosis for my father wasn't good. Given his age and the severity of his injuries, they were doubtful he'd recover enough to regain the use of his legs.

Even then, my mamma didn't break down. It was her strength that made me determined not to fall apart either. My papà was a proud man who needed us to be brave so he could be too.

"You will return to university," my mother said, startling me.

"Now is not the time for us to worry about that, Mamma."

She shook her head emphatically. "You will return."

"You and Papà need me now."

"What your father needs is to know you will be able to take over the winery operations. You cannot do so without finishing your education."

"Mamma, perhaps it would be best if we hired someone to take over permanently."

She held up her hand. "No. You'll finish school, and then you'll come back and run Valentini for your father."

"Mateo could—"

"No," she said a second time.

Mateo Casavetti was the second oldest son of my father's sister. His father had inherited his family's estate and winery in the same way most families did—from his father. When he died, the estate would be passed down to Antonio, Mateo's older brother.

When I was much younger, I remember hearing my parents talk about the future of Valentini. My father always said it would make the most sense for the estate to eventually be passed down to Mateo.

"Mamma, when you and Papà used to talk about Mateo one day inheriting the estate and winery, you said something about your grandmother." I remembered more of what she said, only because it equally thrilled and frightened me. Her words were something like, "It is Pia's birthright, and should you suggest otherwise, the curse of Estancia Valentini will be carried out by future generations until the end of time." Perhaps, in my memory, it was far more dramatic than it had actually been.

"Come with me." My mother led me out of the hospital and into the nearby gardens. "It was actually my *sixth* great-grandmother," she said as we sat side by side on the stone bench. "Her father was the Count of Valentini. When he died, Estancia was his only heir."

"Go on."

"She was…a force of nature, and when someone tried to steal her property from her, she would not stand for it. You know the Valentinis descended from the female line of the Medicis, yes?"

I shook my head. No. I'd had no idea.

"At the time, Italy was divided. The Habsburgs of Austria controlled one portion; the House of Savoy, most of the other. Italy was very poor; the Valentinis, on the other hand, were not."

I rubbed my temples, trying to figure out where in the world my mother was going with this story.

"Legend is, in exchange for giving the House of Savoy half of the family fortune, Estancia became the Countess of Valentini and remained such even after she married for the second time."

"What about the curse, Mamma?"

"*Sì.* Estancia did not marry wisely the first time around. Her husband attempted to take control of the estate to ensure it was passed down to his oldest son from another marriage, rather than the daughter Estancia bore him." My mamma raised a brow. "Her husband met a gruesome demise shortly after she discovered his treachery. It is said she made a public prophecy, stating that anyone who attempted to alter the lineage of the rightful heir by skipping over the oldest child—male or female—would be met with a similar fate."

"That is known as the curse of Estancia Valentini?"

My mamma nodded her head slowly and looked at me with wide eyes.

"What happened to the other half of the family fortune?" It had to have been astronomical wealth if half of it bailed out the finances of an entire country.

"No one knows."

"You don't think Papà's accident…"

She shook her head and then patted my hand and winked. "He saw the error of his ways many years ago, and there was never talk of Mateo inheriting again."

Despite my mamma's protests, I didn't return to university that semester. Instead, I promised I would the next.

My father's recovery was slow and painful, both for him and for us. He was terribly depressed to the point where he had little interest in anything. Each morning, my mother and I would get him into his wheelchair and take him out to the *terrazza* so he could look out over the vineyards. Nonna Bella would make his favorite pastries for breakfast, but more often than not, he said he had no appetite. I was terribly worried about him, as was my mamma.

The police investigated my father's accident, and like with the thefts, they didn't come up with a theory as to what had happened or any suspects.

Without his oversight, wine sales were faltering. I was in a state of constant worry over him, as well as the future of Valentini. While I didn't talk to anyone about it, I was also worried about Mylos.

There were reports of deaths of coalition soldiers every week. If it weren't for my conversations with Lily, in which she assured me they'd hear immediately if anything happened to him, I was sure I'd lose my mind.

I'd always had a hard time keeping weight on, even when I was a little girl, but it got worse. Since Mylos and I were last together, I'd lost so much weight, my clothes were baggy.

"I've been looking for you," said my mamma, coming into the winery office and finding me staring blankly out the window. I turned my chair to face her. "Your papà made a decision."

"Okay."

"He's hired Paolo Viticcio to run the winery while you finish college."

I groaned. "Paolo?"

"*Sì,*" she said, patting my hand.

I still hadn't forgiven him for telling Mylos he was my fiancé. When I'd confronted him about it, he said it was all harmless fun. Something had stopped me that day from telling him how much Mylos meant to me, as if doing so might expose him to some other form of "harmless fun," on Paolo's part.

"Why him, Mamma? Why not Mateo?"

"Your father trusts him, Pia. His family's winery is bigger and more successful than Valentini. He can help us grow, and then when you come back, maybe you and he—"

I shook my head. "I will not marry Paolo. You and Papà need to accept that and stop pushing us together."

"We'll see." She stood and walked out. A few minutes later, Lucia walked in.

"What can I do for you?"

Lucia shook her head and covered my hand with hers. "The question is, what can we do for you?"

"What do you mean?"

"We're all worried about you, Pia. You can't keep this up. You need help."

"We can't afford—"

"I'm not suggesting you hire someone, Pia. There are many here on the estate, in Val d'Orcia, even in your own family, who would be willing to lend support if you'd only let them."

"I can't take advantage—"

"Your family has been more than generous to mine for generations. I'm not the only person who feels that way. Most everyone who works here does."

"I appreciate you saying that, but…"

"I've done something you might not like, but I want you to hear me out before you argue with me."

I took a deep breath and let it out slowly. "What did you do, Lucia?"

"I called Mateo."

"My cousin Mateo?" My eyebrows shot up.

She nodded. "He'll be here this afternoon. He can help run the winery so you can go back to Siena."

"Oh dear."

"What?"

"My mamma just told me my father hired Paolo Viticcio to do the same thing."

"Paolo?" She made a face.

"That was my reaction."

"Sorry, Pia, no offense. I know you and Paolo are—"

"We're nothing. My parents are unwilling to listen when I tell them I'll never marry him."

"If things don't work out, please consider talking with Mateo. He's a good man, Pia."

"You know Mateo cannot inherit Valentini, right?"

She laughed. "You need sleep, my friend. No one is suggesting he inherit. He only wants to support you."

"But what would be in it for him? We can't afford to hire another person to help run the winery."

"Pia, listen to yourself. Do you think so little of the rest of us that you would assume the only reason we would help you is if there were something 'in it for us'?"

"That isn't what I meant." Or maybe it was. Was I being as prideful as my father?

"Mateo would do it out of the goodness of his heart."

For the first time since she mentioned his name, I looked into Lucia's eyes. How did she know what kind of man Mateo was? When she smiled and her cheeks turned pink, I had my answer.

"Are you and my cousin together?"

She half shrugged. "We're trying to be. If both of us were working here, we'd be able to spend more time together. You know, when we aren't working."

I pressed my fingers to my temples, feeling a little like I was losing my grasp on reality. "Lucia, forgive me for asking this, but do you work here?"

She laughed. "Work is a term that can mean many things. While I'm not a Valentini employee, I have been assisting my mother and Nonna Bella."

I gasped. "Why didn't you say anything? You can't just 'assist.' We need to pay you."

"Have you heard a word I've said to you?"

"Yes…no…I don't know."

Her cell phone vibrated, and she looked at the screen. "Mateo's here." She stood to leave, and I put my hand on her arm.

"Please tell him how sorry I am."

"He isn't going to turn around and leave, Pia. You can talk to him yourself."

"Of course. How do you think Georgio is going to react to Paolo being here?"

She shrugged. "You shouldn't care what he thinks. He's a winemaker. What happens with winery operations isn't up to him."

I sensed something was as off between her and Georgio as it was between him and me. It seemed we couldn't talk to each other without it ending in an argument. I didn't know how to make things better between us. Something told me that Paolo taking over, even temporarily, was going to make it much worse.

"Hey," said Georgio, coming into the office moments after Lucia walked out.

"Hi," I said, rubbing my eyes.

"You look like shit."

"Thanks."

"Sorry, but it's true."

I stood, walked over to where he leaned against the desk, and sat next to him. I bumped him with my shoulder. "What happened to us, Georgio? It seems like all we do is fight. We used to be friends. Closer than that. You've always been like a brother to me."

I could feel his body tense. "You remember that? I thought you'd forgotten."

"What are you talking about?"

"We aren't friends anymore, Pia."

"We aren't? Since when?"

"Since we were teenagers."

"I wasn't aware I was no longer your friend."

"Right. You come home; you go back to college. I never know when you'll be here. You don't even say goodbye when you leave. You don't call unless you're checking on a production issue or can't reach anyone else to send you sales reports. You're just like your father."

"What does that mean?"

"To you, I'm just the help."

His words hurt. "I don't feel that way about you, Georgio. I promise I don't. I'm sorry if I've made you feel that way."

"Too little, too late, Pia." He stormed out, slamming the door behind him before I'd had the chance to tell him about my father hiring Paolo.

7

Grinder
Six Months Later
Najaf, Iraq

Yesterday, I turned twenty-two. Other than Keon—Edge—no one made mention of it. I was surprised he did. How did I celebrate? With my twentieth direct kill. I had been indirectly responsible for countless others.

It had been twenty months since Edge and I were deployed to Iraq on a secret mission to locate and take out certain members of the Iraqi military, supposedly our allies but, in reality, responsible for innumerable coalition deaths.

I hated everything about this fucking place. It wasn't just the searing heat of the desert that made me and the rest of the men I served with miserable bastards; we were supposed to be back home by now. After eighteen months spent in a country where I felt like I'd been transported back to the Middle Ages, I was beyond ready to get the hell out of here.

Four days before our scheduled transport, Sunni insurgents staged three uprisings, undoing months of work spent training Iraqi forces, and sending the region right back into chaos and instability.

The men in the coalition platoon Edge and I were placed in were from the US as well as the UK. Our unit made up what was known as a Quick Reaction Force— or QRF. We stood ready to respond at a moment's notice in the event another unit was attacked or needed help.

It was a little before midnight when we got the call ordering us on a mission to clear insurgents out of Sadr City, a dense Shiite area in eastern Baghdad. Edge and I also received intel that a top lieutenant in the Mahdi Army had been seen in the area in the last twenty-four hours.

We split into teams and piled into the armored personnel carriers known as BFVs—Bradley Fighting Vehicles—and moved out. It wasn't long after we pushed into the streets of the city that we went under fire from rocket-propelled grenades and AK-47s. There were nine of us in the vehicle: the commander, the gunner, and me, tonight's designated driver. The six other men were crammed into a small hold in the rear of the tank. The hammer of rifle fire against metal and the explosive charges of the rocket-propelled grenades was ear-shattering.

I was attempting to maneuver into a position where our hatch could be lowered and the soldiers in the tank could dismount, when the BFV hit an improvised explosive device. The last thing I remembered was being blown out of the hatch and landing on the ground, my body engulfed in a ball of flames.

I lost consciousness but came to every so often, for a few seconds at a time, certain I was dead, since I couldn't feel any pain. I could hear Edge's voice, but before I could decipher his words, everything would fade back to black.

I vaguely remember the helicopter transport, mainly because it was the first time I felt any real pain. The jostling is what made me come to; the subsequent pain sent me back under.

"Captain Stone," I heard a woman's voice repeating. I opened my eyes. "Ah, there he is. Do you know where you are, Captain Stone?"

Based on her accent, I would guess Germany, and by the medical equipment surrounding me, a hospital. "Not really," I answered.

"You're in the Burn Intensive Care Unit of the GER Armed Forces Central Military Hospital in Koblenz, Germany."

"Right," I said, closing my eyes.

"What number would you give your pain presently?"

"On a scale of?"

"One to ten."

"Zero."

"Captain Stone, are you still with me?"

"Yes." I opened my eyes, wishing she'd just go away and leave me the hell alone.

"The doctor has been waiting to talk to you."

She walked out, and I let my eyes drift closed again.

"Captain Stone?" This time it was a man's voice.

I opened my eyes.

"I'm Dr. Schweitzer. How are you doing?" he asked with the same strong German accent.

"You tell me, Doc."

He pulled a chair over and sat in it. "Do you remember what happened to you?"

I shook my head. I was groggy, but something inside warned me I wouldn't want to pull whatever we were about to discuss to the forefront of my consciousness.

"You suffered third-degree burns on approximately thirty percent of your body—your lower left torso and your left leg primarily."

"You must be giving me some bloody good pain meds, Doc."

He slowly closed his eyes and reopened them. "With a burn such as yours, which we classify as full-thickness, the dermis is completely destroyed. You may feel sensations of pressure, but no nerve endings remain to transport the feeling of pain to your brain."

"How long have I been here?"

"About sixteen days."

"The last thing I remember…" I couldn't go on.

"You were kept in a medically induced coma to prevent you from further injuring yourself."

"I wouldn't mind if you put me back under."

He nodded. "I understand, but there are a few people here who are waiting to see you. I asked that they let me explain your injuries and treatment plan before they came in."

I closed my eyes again, certain I didn't want to hear what he was about to tell me.

I listened only superficially as he explained different types of skin grafts, which were temporary, and which could be considered permanent.

"It will take approximately one month for the grafts to heal."

"You're saying I'll be out of here in a few weeks' time?"

Dr. Schweitzer shook his head. "With the amount of skin that will need to be grafted, it will take several surgeries. You will be with us for at least one year, Miles. Is it okay if I call you Miles?"

I could barely register his question; my mind was swirling with his prediction that I'd be here a year. *At least.*

"Before I bring your parents in, do you have any further questions at this time?"

Fighting tears, I found my voice. "Just one."

"Go ahead."

"Why the fuck did you let me live?"

When he stood to leave, I called out to him.

"Yes?"

"I don't want them to see me like this."

"If you mean your injuries, they've seen you, Miles. They've been here every day since you arrived."

I turned my head, fighting threatening tears. "I don't want to see them. I don't want to see anyone. I want to be left the hell alone."

The doctor's already solemn expression grew more somber. "I understand, Miles, but the support of your family is essential to your recovery."

I didn't respond. I'd told him I didn't want to see anyone. Whether he respected my wishes or not, there was nothing I could do about it. It wasn't as if I could get up and walk out of the room.

A few minutes later, the door opened and my mum and dad came in. They both put on a brave face, but their cheeks were tear-stained and their eyes red and swollen.

Mum stood beside me and brushed the hair from my forehead. "The most important thing I want to say to you, is to tell you how much I love you. I thank God every day that you're still with us."

Did she know I wished for the exact opposite? Had she been listening to my conversation with the doctor?

"Miles," said my father, standing on the other side of the bed. "Son..." His eyes filled with tears, and he looked away.

The door opened again, and a woman walked in who looked like my sister but with an extra five stone. When she rested her hand on her stomach, I realized she was pregnant.

"Hi," she said, coming to take my father's place.

"You look big as a house."

She smiled through her tears. "Sure, go on, then, make fun of me when I can't give you a swat for it."

"How many do you have in there?"

"Just one, and it seems he'll be born here in Germany."

"He?"

"That's right." She clenched her eyes and gripped the bed rail. "Sorry," she said a few seconds later. "Contractions."

Several hours later, according to my nurse, Angus Miles Spencer was born in the hospital adjacent to the burn center.

My mum and dad were gone for quite a while, and I appreciated the respite, as short-lived as it was.

I had no idea what to expect when the male nurse came in to tell me it was time for a dressing change.

"This won't be easy," he said. "You might do better if you don't look. At least in the beginning."

"Wait." I put my hand on his when he went to move the bedclothes. "The doc said 'lower left torso.' What does that mean?"

He put his hand near his hipbone. "You're burned from here around to your backside."

"What about the front?"

"Looks about the same as your arm." He nudged me.

"Thanks. What's your name?"

"Carson, and you'll be right sick of me in no time."

"You're English?"

Carson nodded. "Your mum and dad made arrangements for me to begin your rehab here. That way, when you return to England, there will be a continuum of care."

"Bloody hell! What's that cost?"

"I reckon not as much as you're worth to them."

After giving me a hefty pump of morphine and applying analgesics to the left lower portion of my body and my leg, Carson began the process of changing my dressings. I took his advice and didn't allow myself to look.

When he finished what I can only describe as pain worse than a thousand knives stuck into my muscles, and that was with the pain meds, I was wrung out.

Evidently, there were more than a few nerve endings still functioning well enough to talk to my brain.

"Get some rest," Carson said, patting my shoulder. "I'll be back tomorrow."

I rested my head against the pillow. "I'd rather you not."

I was a week in and preparing for my second skin graft surgery. They'd performed the first right after I arrived, while I was in the medically induced coma.

Carson was in the midst of a dressing change when the door to my room opened and Edge walked in.

"Aren't you a sight?" he said, clapping me on the shoulder. "How the hell are you, Grind?"

Carson raised his head. "Who's this?"

"Edge, this is Carson, aka Mengele."

"You wanker, how many times do I need to remind you we're in Germany, for fuck's sake?" he spat under his breath.

Calling Carson Mengele was only one of the ways I paid him back for the pain he put me through on a daily basis.

I allowed almost no one else in to see me. Even the nurses knew not to initiate unnecessary conversation after I'd systematically berated them to the point where they must have taken to drawing straws to see who would be forced to come in and take my vitals.

He finished up and left Edge and me on our own.

"I'm sorry it's taken me so long to get here. I put in for leave straightaway."

I held up my hand. "You don't need to feel like you have to be here." When his eyes scrunched, I felt like an absolute tosser. "Look, I know you mean well by coming, but I'd prefer to be alone."

"I'm sorry, Miles."

"I told you, I know you mean well. I just—"

"Not for coming." He scrubbed his face with his hand. "I should've been driving that BFV."

"By way of what?"

He shook his head. "I just should have been."

I didn't respond. What could I say? We both knew it was the luck of the draw. I wouldn't wish what happened to me on my worst enemy, let alone my best friend.

"Whatever I can do…"

"I appreciate it, but—" The door opened again, and this time, a woman walked in. *The woman.* What the hell was Pia doing here?

"Am I interrupting?"

"No," said Edge at the same time I said, "Yes."

"I can come back later."

Edge stood and walked toward the door. "I'll give you a few minutes."

When Pia walked closer to the bed, I closed my eyes. I didn't want her here. I didn't want her to see me like this, but more, I didn't want to see her pity reflected back at me if I looked into her eyes.

"You shouldn't be here."

"I had to come."

I opened my eyes and stared her down. "Why?"

The question appeared to stun her. "I care about you, Mylos."

"You shouldn't be here," I repeated. "I don't want you here." I turned my head and closed my eyes. "Leave, Pia."

"But, Mylos, I left school, I traveled—"

"I don't care. I asked you to leave, and I'd appreciate it if you'd have enough respect for me to do so."

I didn't open my eyes again until long after I heard the door close behind her. I had no idea who had contacted her or suggested she visit, but I'd make it abundantly clear to everyone that I wouldn't permit her to come back.

8

Pia

I walked out of Mylos' room and leaned against the wall outside his door as silent sobs racked my body. The beautiful man-boy I knew was gone. It had nothing to do with his injuries; it was his heart I could no longer feel. I longed to wrap my arms around him and give him comfort. Instead, I wrapped my arms around my own waist. I couldn't describe the pain I experienced when he said he didn't want me there, when he told me to leave.

"Ma'am?" I heard a man's voice say. "Pia?"

I raised my head and wiped at my tears.

"I'm Keon."

"I'm sorry," I said, trying to square my shoulders and stop my tears. I was about to introduce myself but then realized he'd called me by name.

"Mylos—Miles—and I…" I couldn't go on.

"He says your name sometimes in his sleep." He put his arm around my shoulders.

Part of me wanted to know if Mylos had ever told him about me. The other part didn't want to know what he might've said.

"If it makes you feel any better, I'm his best friend and he doesn't want me here either." He smiled, but then the look on his face grew serious. "Knowing Miles the way I do, my guess is he doesn't want any of us here. You, me, his sister, or his parents. I know him to be a private and very proud man. Having to depend on others will never be easy for him."

I nodded, unsurprised by his friend's assessment.

"If you want to give me your number, I can call you if anything changes," the man offered.

As in, if he asked for me? That would never happen. I might as well walk out of the hospital and return to Italy. But I wasn't here only for him. Lily had asked me to come. I would give her the comfort and support her brother refused from me.

"That's very nice of you," I said when he handed me his phone and I put my number in it. "Thank you."

I walked to the elevator, turning once more before I pressed the button. Mylos' friend was still staring at me. What was he thinking? I wondered. When I heard the elevator's ding, I held up my hand, and he did the same.

When I exited in the lobby, I saw Mylos' mother and father sitting in the atrium. Not sure whether Lily told them she'd contacted me, I didn't walk over to speak with them. As I passed by, headed toward the exit, Margaret, Lily and Mylos' mother, called out to me.

"Pia," she cried, drawing me into a hug. "I'm so glad you've come. Have you seen Miles?"

I thought about lying and saying I didn't go in, because his friend was there. "I didn't stay, since he had company." Still a lie.

"Yes, well, Edge is his best friend, and he's just arrived. That was so thoughtful of you, dear."

I took a step back, out of her embrace. "I'll come back later."

"Where are you staying? We're across the way at the Sofitel."

"I…um…am staying with friends of our family." That was a lie too; I was staying in the same hotel they were.

"Oh, that's nice. Is it close by?"

"Not too far." I took another step back. "I'll see you soon, yes?"

Margaret looked perplexed. "You don't want to wait with us?"

"I have an errand to run, but then I'll come back. Okay?"

That seemed to appease her.

"We'll all have dinner later, then."

I cringed once my back was turned. Soon enough, she'd know her son didn't want me here.

I waited until long after visiting hours were over before going back to the hospital. I sneaked past the security guard and ducked into the restroom. I waited a few minutes, came out, and walked to the bank of elevators.

No one stopped me until I was about to walk into the burn center.

"Excuse me, who are you here to see?" asked a woman seated behind a desk.

"Mylos…Miles…Stone."

"And you are?"

"Pia Deltetto." Before I could say anything more, she stood, walked around the desk, and took my hand.

"*You're* Pia. I wondered. He talks about you sometimes in his sleep." It was the same thing his friend had said earlier. "You must be very important to him.

I'll waive the rules this time." She winked and walked back behind the desk.

I slowly opened the door to his room, relieved to see he was asleep. As quietly as I could, I sat in the chair by his bedside. If nothing else, I could look at him, breathe the same air he did. He shifted his body slightly and opened his hand. There, in his palm, rested the heart-shaped stone I'd sent to him.

I must've dozed off in the chair, but woke when I heard voices coming from the hallway. I grabbed my bag and sneaked out as quietly as I could, praying Mylos didn't wake up.

I checked the time; it was one in the morning. I'd been in the room with him for almost three hours. Most of which I spent sleeping.

The street was still as I walked across to my hotel.

I'd get a good night's rest and maybe try to see Mylos again tomorrow. Knowing he still had my stone gave me hope that he didn't hate me quite as much as I believed he did.

I opened the door to my room and flicked on the switch. The light on the phone was blinking red, indicating I had a message waiting. I called the front desk.

"Ms. Deltetto, yes, we have several urgent messages for you."

"From?"

"Paolo Viticcio. He said it is imperative he speak with you as soon as possible."

Without returning Paolo's call, I knew. I could feel it in my heart. My beloved papà was gone.

9

Grinder
Two Years Later
London, England

After two years in the Koblenz Burn Center, I was finally home.

A little over a month ago, I'd had my last skin graft surgery, at least for now. There was always the chance a particular area may need more work. Risk of infection was also something I dealt with on a daily basis, although at the six-month mark of any graft, odds of that happening went down significantly.

With each graft, the pain got worse instead of better. What used to work well enough to alleviate it, no longer did.

With the exception of Carson, my caregivers encouraged me to seek and try alternative pain management. How the hell was I supposed to meditate my pain away when it hurt so bad I couldn't think?

I'd made plans to meet up with Edge at the local pub at half-past four, but showed up an hour early. I was on my second pint by the time he arrived.

I stood when I saw him walk in. The stress of seeing me again was evident in the lines on his face.

Neither of us spoke as he approached. We embraced with the requisite back slaps and then stepped apart.

"Fancy a pint?" I asked, motioning to the bar.

"I wouldn't mind something stronger to chase it."

"I'm right there with you, mate."

He looked left and right and then rubbed the back of his neck.

"What's bothering you?"

"Would you mind if we went to my flat?"

Knowing the pub was a regular stop for many who worked at SIS, I immediately understood his concern. "Not at all."

A little over an hour later, we were both bladdered. Edge stood, presumably to pour us each another shot of Irish. I got up to join him and saw him fingering the red stone I'd inadvertently left on the counter. I reached over and put it in the pocket of my trousers.

"Where did you get that?"

Pia was a topic of discussion I avoided. Not just with Edge, but with everyone. "Long story," I said, downing one shot and pouring another.

"We're too pissed to go anywhere, so you might as well tell me."

I sat back down and looked up at the ceiling. "When I was sixteen, I went to Italy with my parents…"

"Blooming hell," he said when I got to the part where Pia came to the hospital and I told her to leave.

I shook my head, reached into my pocket, and took out the heart-shaped stone. "She never came back. As much as I told myself I didn't want her to, part of me was disappointed."

"I'm surprised she didn't, especially after…"

"What?"

"Nothing."

"You bloody bastard. I just told you my whole life story."

"It wasn't anything she said specifically. I just got the impression she was in love with you."

I laughed. "Infatuation. Nothing more."

"She's done a number on you."

No more than I had on her.

"You need to get your mind off her. Find someone else, even just for a shag."

I groaned, hating that Edge brought up anything to do with sex, especially after we'd just finished talking about Pia—who I still fantasized about both awake and in my dreams.

It had been a long time since I was with a woman. First, it was because we were in Iraq for fourteen months. Then…well…I couldn't imagine any woman would want me now. Not that it was something I'd discuss with Edge.

It wasn't just the scarring, which in itself would be horrifying. Everything about my time in Iraq had changed something in me. I didn't go a single night without nightmares.

In most of them, I relived the explosion and being on fire. In some, though, I dreamed about the last man I killed before that mission. I knew I'd never forget the way his eyes had remained fixated on mine, even in death.

I looked up from my drink, and Edge was studying me.

"You love her too."

I shook my head. "You're wrong."

"Good morning, son," said my father, joining me in the kitchen the following day.

"Morning." I scrubbed my face with my hand. "Listen, I really appreciate you and Mum letting me stay here."

When he raised his head, the look in his eyes almost shattered me. I'd been the worst son imaginable through my ordeal, the worst person, really.

I lashed out so much at those who cared about me, it was a wonder they ever spoke to me again. The only person I didn't seem to faze was Carson. It didn't matter what kind of abuse I hurled at him; it slid off his back, and he went on as though I hadn't said a word. He also counseled my parents as to how to deflect my anger, but having their son turn into the devil incarnate had worn them down.

"You don't need to thank us, Miles. Your mum and I love you. We'd do anything for you."

Including blow through their entire life savings to provide for a private combination of nurse and care-giver. The settlement I got from the British Army had replenished their reserves. My promise to never speak to either of them again if they refused the money was the only thing that made them finally relent and accept it. As it was, I still had three times as much money in the bank as they did. I'd give them every penny if they'd let me; however, even I knew there may come a day when I'd need it for further medical care.

"Your sister is stopping by later this morning."

I nodded. Yet another person who had suffered my abuse. She and William had plans to be married shortly before the explosion that had altered the course of my life forever. It had been planned to coincide with my leave from deployment, but given that had been canceled, they decided to get married by the local magistrate rather than have the elaborately planned wedding.

Now that I was back in London, there were plans for a combined celebration: homecoming for me and a wedding party for them. Tonight, in fact. There was nothing I wanted to participate in less. No one should be celebrating my homecoming. No one should be celebrating me at all.

What few talked about, including my best friend, was that I was not the only person injured in the explosion of the IED I'd driven the BFV onto. Of the nine in the vehicle that night, two had escaped with minor injuries, four were dead, one had lost his leg, and one had such severe brain damage he'd never lead a normal life. And there was me. The one responsible, still living a life I had no desire to.

It remained a daily struggle to open my eyes and get out of bed. I alternated between believing my family would be better off without the burden I'd become and believing that killing myself would leave them shells of their former selves.

Carson, my torturer and my protector, lost his temper with me only once. After hours of my constant complaining, self-pity, and unrelenting talk of ending my life, he'd had enough. Among many other things, he called me the most selfish, self-pitying, piece-of-shit wanker he'd ever had the displeasure of knowing.

"Instead of feeling sorry for yourself day in, day out, you could be helping others who have suffered in the same way you have. Do you not realize there are *children* in the pediatric burn center at Chelsea who could benefit from seeing where you're at now compared to where you started?"

He'd walked out on me that day only to return the next as though we hadn't had a foul word pass between us. When I met with my therapist later that week, he echoed many of the things Carson had said to me but with fewer curse words. He also suggested that helping others may help me find my self-worth again.

I still hadn't looked into volunteering at Chelsea. The idea of it terrified me. What if my darkness was the only thing they saw? What if instead of helping, I made their already impossible struggles more difficult?

"I'm going for a walk," I said, grabbing my jacket.

"Miles?" said my father.

"Yeah?"

"Did you not hear me say your sister would be stopping by?"

"Don't worry. I won't be long." I walked out, knowing without needing to look that he was shaking his head in disappointment.

I was about to go through the front gate when my sister approached.

"Trying to avoid me?"

"Isn't you."

"I know. It's yourself you're trying to get away from."

"Where's Angus?"

"With Wills."

I nodded. My nephew was terrified of me. I knew that. What child wouldn't be? It was one of the reasons I didn't take Carson's suggestion to volunteer at Chelsea.

My sister put her hand on my arm. "Miles, we're all so worried about you."

I shrugged away from her. "Don't be. I'm not worth the energy."

"Don't say things like that."

I looked down at the ground. "I say it, Lil, because it's true."

Before I realized what she was about to do, she put her arms around my waist in a near-death grip. "Do you have any idea how I felt when we thought we might lose you? Any idea? I wouldn't have been able to go on, Miles. Mum and Dad felt the same way. You may not feel like it, but you're the light of our lives, little brother. Not that you're so little anymore, but, God, how can you not know how much we love you?"

My eyes filled with tears, and I looked away. "Lily…"

"Can we go inside? It's mighty chilly out here," she said a few minutes later.

I thought about telling her I still needed the walk, but after her admission, I owed her some of my attention.

Also, the left side of my body ached from the cold. It was a toss-up as to which doctor would say it was my imagination and which would prescribe rehabilitation to combat it. It seemed their opinions changed on a regular basis.

"Oh, good. You're back," said my father when Lily and I came in the front door.

"Never left, actually."

Dad took a drink of his tea and looked between my sister and me. Something was up; that was obvious.

"I'll just be checking on your mum, then," he said before walking out of the kitchen.

"Get to it, Lil. What's going on?"

When she bit her bottom lip, I knew it was something big.

"Two things, actually."

"Yes?"

"First, I'm pregnant."

"That's bloody brilliant." I smiled and hugged her.

"And…the second you might not be as happy about, but before you decide to be a wanker about it, remember this party is as much for Wills and me as it is for you."

I motioned for her to go on.

"Pia is coming."

"I see." I grabbed the back of the chair. "Lily, I…"

"My party too, Miles. And Wills'."

It wasn't that I didn't want to see her. I did. Desperately so. What I wasn't so certain about was how she might react to seeing me.

"Excuse me." I went upstairs, pulled my prescription pack out of the bag, and opened the lid of one of several bottles. My modus operandi when it came to my pain management became: if one is good, more are better. I dumped a handful of the small white pills into my palm, tossed them in my mouth, and swallowed. When I came out of my room and walked around the corner, I saw Lily leaning up against the wall, arms crossed.

"What the fuck, Miles?"

"Let it go, Lily."

"The hell, I will." She scooted around me, grabbed my bag, and pulled out my prescription pack. The only way I could get it from her would be to hurt her, and even in my compromised state of thinking, I wouldn't do that.

"Does Carson know about all this?"

"It's none of your business."

"The hell, it isn't."

"What's going on in here?" said my father, coming down the hallway.

"This," she said, pointing to the various bottles the pack held, and reminding me of what a tattler she'd been when we were wee ones.

My father's eyes met mine, and in them, I saw the same pain I had so many times before, only now it was so much worse. He rubbed the back of his neck. "I've never felt like such a failure as a father and as a man."

His words nearly floored me. I stumbled backwards, landing on the bed I'd slept in since childhood.

"It isn't you, Dad. It's nothing to do with you."

He sat down next to me. "You are flesh of my flesh. How can this have nothing to do with me? You're an extension of me. Both you and your sister. Of your mum too."

"Don't get Mum involved in this. I beg you."

"I can't lie to her. I won't."

"What's this?" My mum came in and sat on the other side of me.

"Miles is abusing his painkillers," said Lily, pointing to the bag in the same way she had with my father.

I don't know what I expected, but it wasn't for my mother to take my hand in hers and say, "Of course he is, Lily."

My sister's mouth hung open in the same way I'm sure mine did.

"What we must do now is help him find better ways of managing it."

My head snapped up when I heard a knock on the front door. "Who's that?"

"I told you, Miles," said Lily. "Pia is here."

I ran my hand through my hair. When Lily started for the stairs, I called out to her. "Let me, Lil." I stood and rounded the corner to find my sister staring at me with wide eyes. "Whatever you're afraid I'll do, I won't."

10

Pia

It had been two years since Mylos kicked me out of his hospital room. Two years since I sat by his bedside and watched him sleep without him knowing I was there.

In that time, I'd finally graduated, with a degree in viticulture and enology with an emphasis on wine business and marketing.

Once I reached my degree-level classes, I was surprised by how much I already knew just from growing up at Valentini. So many practices I'd watched my father implement, by intuition alone, were applied principles of my education.

It had also been as long since my papà died. The doctors said he'd had a heart attack, but I think it was more that his heart was broken. Day after day, he'd sit on the *terrazza* and look out over his beloved vineyards, knowing he'd never walk them again.

As hard as it was for me to admit, Paolo had been a godsend, and while Valentini was still struggling, at least we hadn't gone bankrupt.

Since I returned from college, I'd taken over most of the day-to-day operations while also trying to come up with alternative income streams for Valentini. Paolo checked in often, offering his help, but so far, I hadn't needed it. He was also relentless in his romantic pursuit of me. I knew each time I turned him down, he was hurt, but I couldn't think about things like dating now. I had too much to do to make sure my family's livelihood remained viable.

When Lily invited me to come this weekend, I hesitated, but Lucia convinced me the short break would do me good. She said that Mateo would be visiting, and if anything came up, he would be there to help.

My cousin and Lucia spent as much time as they could together. After my father died, there was less housework to be done at Valentini, so she wasn't there as often. I'd even suggested to Nonna Carina that she didn't have to work every day, but she and Nonna Bella still arrived at Valentini every morning to take care of my mamma and me.

I'm here for Lily. The mantra had played over and over in my mind since I stepped off the plane and now, as I stood outside the Stone residence, willing myself to walk up to the front door just like I had the first time I visited.

Finally, after several minutes, I forced myself to take a few more steps, raised my hand, and knocked.

The last person I expected to see when the door opened was Mylos. I covered my heart with my hand and stared into his beautiful brown eyes.

"Hi."

"Pia, come in."

"I'm not intruding?"

He smiled, nearly melting my heart. "You're an invited guest. You'd hardly be intruding."

I took several deep breaths and followed him inside.

"Is your family at home?" I asked as he took my coat and hung it in the closet.

"They're upstairs."

"Oh." I bit my bottom lip and winced.

"They're giving us time." He led me into the front sitting room. "Can I get you anything?"

"No, thank you." I sat on the sofa and folded my hands in my lap, not remembering the last time I felt this nervous. Mylos sat in a chair across from me.

"How are you?" we both asked at the same time and then laughed.

"Go ahead."

"No, you first, Pia."

"I'm fine. I graduated."

He leaned forward and rested his elbows on his knees. "I'm really proud of you."

"Thank you. There were a lot of stops and starts—" I cut my sentence short when it dawned on me he might think I meant because of him. "My father had an accident."

"I heard he passed away. I'm so sorry, Pia."

"Thank you. It was for the best; he was in a lot of pain—" I did it again. I was trying too hard, and because of it, I was stumbling over my words. "I miss him very much."

"How long are you in town?"

"Just a few days. You know, for the party tonight."

He sighed. "Right. The party."

"You'd rather not attend?"

He took a deep breath and blew it out. "I'd love to attend the celebration of my sister and her husband."

"Everyone there would welcome you back anyway. Celebrate your return."

"I'm not great at being the center of attention. At least not anymore." He shook his head. "I'm not sure I ever was."

I couldn't take my eyes off him. He looked so good compared to the last time I saw him. His hair, longer than I'd ever seen it, fell onto his forehead. His beard was longer too, covering the lower half of his face. His eyes, though, their warmth were my undoing. It was such a relief to see after how cold they'd been when I saw him in Germany. My chest ached just from looking at him. My fingers longed to feel him. My body craved his touch.

"Pia…the way you're looking at me…"

My gaze drifted to the floor, and my cheeks heated in shame. "Forgive me," I whispered.

"I thought I heard voices down here," said Margaret, rushing into the room. I stood and we embraced. "I'm so happy to see you, Pia."

"Me too," I murmured.

Mylos' father, John, hugged me too and then stepped back so Lily and I could embrace.

"Thank you so much for being here," she whispered. "It means everything."

"I wouldn't have missed it."

"Are you sure I can't talk you into staying with Wills and me? Angus sleeps through the night now."

"I appreciate it so much, but I brought work with me that I really must take care of early tomorrow morning."

"Sounds like an excuse to me, but I'll stop pestering you. I'm off now to go home and get ready. Can I drop you at your hotel?"

"Pia, you don't need to rush off so fast, do you?" asked Margaret.

"Mum, she'll see you all tonight, and then she'll be here for a few days." Lily looked at me. "Right?"

"Yes. A couple."

"Let her rest, and she'll see you later."

My eyes met Mylos', and I raised my hand. He did the same. "See you later?"

He nodded.

"Let's go, then," said Lily, picking up my bag. She rushed out the front door and closed it the minute I stepped out.

"Stop." I held up my hand, but not in the same way I had with Mylos. "Why are you in such a hurry?"

"I desperately need to talk to you."

Lily didn't say anything on the way to the hotel. In fact, it wasn't until I'd checked in and asked the valet to take my bags to the room that she took my hand and led me over to an out-of-the-way alcove. When I sat in one of the chairs, she sat in the other and reached into her bag. She pulled out a zippered case.

"What is that?"

"This is what I need to talk to you about."

I waited as she unzipped it. "These are all Miles'," she said, pulling out pill bottles one by one.

"And? Why do you have them?"

"They're all painkillers, Pia."

I pressed my fingertips to my temples. "The pain he's in must be unimaginable."

"No. You're not understanding. These are all very similar types of drugs."

I reached forward and put my hand on Lily's arm. "I know you must be frustrated with me, but I don't understand."

"Miles is abusing painkillers. I think he may be addicted to opioids."

I tried to process what she was telling me. It was a subject I knew little about and said so.

"I followed him up to his room and stood just outside the door. I saw him open one of these bottles and put a *handful* of pills in his mouth."

"Okay…"

"Read what it says, Pia."

I took the bottle from her hand. "One, every six hours. Up to four a day." I looked into her eyes. "I see. But, Lily, did you take away all his medicine?"

She shook her head. "No. I left one bottle. There were plenty in it."

I continued to rub my temples. There was a reason she was telling me this. I was unsure whether I wanted to know what it was. "What are you going to do?"

"I want you to help me talk him into getting help."

Exactly what I was afraid of. "He won't listen to me, Lily. We…I'm not sure…"

"What?"

"I don't think Mylos and I are even friends anymore. If we ever were."

Lily raised one eyebrow. "You're far more than that, Pia. You're the woman my brother loves."

I went up to my room and lay down on the bed. The party didn't start for another four hours, and I needed every minute to think.

I knew I was incapable of doing what Lily was asking of me. The man hadn't wanted me to see him in the hospital; how would he react if I tried to butt my nose into his business? I knew nothing about what he went through, except what Lily had told me, and most of it, I didn't want to hear.

Knowing how much pain he was in, how grueling his recovery had been and would continue to be, caused my own pain. My heart ached for him. But not only for his pain. My heart ached for him because even though I'd never admit to anyone—not even him—I loved Mylos.

When I thought about my future, or when my mother pestered me about when I was going to give in and marry Paolo, I could never see it happening.

I could never marry another man, knowing that in my heart, Mylos was my one true love. From the beginning, fate kept us apart, maybe to warn us we could never be. But my heart didn't listen. Even if I never saw him again after tonight, I'd love him until the day I died. It would be unfair to let another man think he could own even a sliver of my heart.

I sat up when I heard a knock at my door and looked over at the time. I must've drifted off. The party would be starting in an hour, and I still had to get ready.

"Un momento," I hollered, straightening my clothes and my hair as I walked toward the door. I opened it without looking, stunned for the second time today to see Mylos on the other side.

"What are you doing here?"

"I…um…never mind."

"Wait!" I called out as he rushed down the hallway toward the elevator. I followed, but the door closed behind him before I got there. I stalked back to my room with clenched fists only to find the door had closed behind me. I was locked out.

With a growl, I padded my way, barefoot, back to the elevator, drumming my fingers on my arm. I took it down to the main floor and walked over to the front desk. The line was ten deep.

I stood there, just having rolled out of bed, no shoes on my feet, fuming.

"Damn you, Mylos," I muttered under my breath as I impatiently waited for the line to move. A couple who had been at the front, turned and walked toward me. I couldn't believe my eyes.

"Paolo?"

"Pia? What are you doing here?"

"I'm in town to visit a friend."

"What a funny coincidence," he said, running his hand through his hair. The woman hanging on his arm appeared unamused.

"Hello," I said, looking directly at her, even though she refused to make eye contact with me; she was too busy looking at my toes.

"Sorry. Pia, this is Donnatella. Donnatella, Pia."

"Hello," I said a second time. She gave me an icy nod, but didn't speak. Perhaps she was mute.

"What are you doing here?" Paolo asked a second time, looking down at my feet like the woman hanging on him had.

"As I said, I'm in town to visit a friend."

"No, I mean in the lobby."

I squared my shoulders. I had no reason to be embarrassed in front of these people, but I was. "It's a long story, but I was locked out of my room."

Donnatella shifted her hand so the light would hit what had to be a ten-carat diamond ring.

"Congratulations," I said, looking back at Paolo. "When is the big day?"

"Not for a few months," he answered sheepishly.

"Well, congratulations again."

"It was nice to see you."

I breathed out a sigh of relief when he walked away, only to tense up when I heard him say my name again. "Is there anything I can do? Talk to the manager?"

I looked over to where his fiancée stood scowling at me.

"I'm perfectly capable of talking to the manager myself, Mylos—I mean, Paolo."

He leaned forward and kissed my cheek.

"What was that for?"

"I miss you, Pia, more than you know. *Ciao!*"

"Whatever," I mumbled, turning around to see the line hadn't moved forward at all. I looked at the large clock above the concierge desk. The party would begin in a half hour, and I wouldn't be there.

I turned back toward the front desk when I saw the man beneath the clock stand. "Can I help you with something, miss?" He too looked down at my bare feet.

"Yes. I was locked out of my room."

"Come. You don't have to wait in line."

"Grazie." I would still be late, but not quite as late as I would've been had I been forced to wait.

11

Grinder

"Have you heard from Pia?" my sister asked.

"No. Why would I have?"

"I don't know." She checked the time. "She's late."

"Ring her."

"You could ring her."

"Lily, you're the one who's worried about why she's late. You ring her."

She studied me with scrunched eyes. "Did something happen?"

"What are you talking about?"

"You're acting funny."

I put my arm around my sister's shoulders and led her far enough away that no one could hear us speaking. "I'm acting funny? Do you want to tell me what you did with my medication?"

"It's in a safe place. And I spoke with Carson—"

"Bloody hell, Lily. What the fuck do you think—"

"Problem?" asked Wills, coming up behind me.

"Ask your wife." I stormed off, seriously considering leaving when I saw *her* walk in. It was one of those moments when time seemed to stand still. When Pia's eyes met mine, everyone—everything—in the room faded to nothing as she slowly made her way toward me. God, she was gorgeous. The word itself paled in the face of her.

Her long, flowing gown was the same color as the stone I was never without. The closer she got, the more tempted I was to fall to my knees and beg her to forgive me, beg her to love me. Instead, I stood where I was, anxious to hear what she would say, but then I couldn't wait. "You're late."

I took a step closer so I could breathe in the glorious scent of her as I reached into my pocket and fingered the heart-shaped stone. I ran the tip of my digit over its facets, softly stroking it like I would the folds of her pussy—if only I was capable of being with her in that way.

"It's your fault, Mylos." Her breath hitched as I stared into her eyes. The music began to play; I held out my hand, and she took it.

"Dance with me, Pia." I wrapped my arm around her waist and pulled her body close to mine. As we floated around the ballroom floor, I rested my cheek against her hair.

"You are just as beautiful—more beautiful—than the day I first saw you outside the window of the farmhouse."

She touched my cheek with the tip of her index finger. "You are beautiful too, Mylos."

"Beautiful? There's so much more to a man than his beauty, Pia."

She laughed as I repeated the words she'd said to me when we met in the village near Valentini.

"There's something I've been meaning to ask you."

"*Sì?*"

"Why is it called *Antica Cascina dei Conti di Valentini* when your last name is Deltetto?"

"Valentini was handed down from my mother's side of the family. She is the Countess Valentini."

"Wow. I had no idea. Is that unusual?"

"As you said, you have no idea."

She took a deep breath and let it out slowly.

"What's wrong, Pia?"

"I don't know how to act around you."

From the corner of my eye, I saw my sister watching us.

"Why did you come to my room earlier? Which, by the way, is why I was late. When I followed you, I locked myself out."

I slowly closed my eyes and opened them. "I'm sorry."

"What happened next bothered me more."

I leaned back to look into her eyes. "What happened?"

"I was standing in the hotel lobby, barefoot like a *zingara*—gypsy—and ran into Paolo."

"Paolo? I'd forgotten all about him."

"Yes, well, I had the good fortune to meet his fiancée, who was not so thrilled to meet me."

"Any woman would be jealous of you, Pia."

"I could understand why: me with no shoes on, very threatening."

I smiled when she did. "I am sorry you had to experience someone unpleasant because of me."

She tapped my shoulder with her hand. "I appreciate your apology, Mylos, but I would much prefer an answer to my question."

"It's not an easy thing to explain."

She was quiet as I continued to move her around the dance floor.

"We didn't get much of a chance to talk when you arrived at my parents' place. There was more I wanted to say."

"Say it now."

"I want you to understand I don't want your pity, Pia. Now or then."

"Then?"

"When you came to Germany."

"And you were certain I would pity you?"

"Let's say it became my expectation."

"I understand."

"What happened to me…There were times, there are times…I don't feel like myself anymore."

She put her hand on my heart and brushed my lips with hers. That brief contact filled me with warmth that quickly turned to something akin to dread. I couldn't allow myself to kiss her. If I did, I'd want more, and I wasn't capable of more.

I saw Edge walk in and nodded to his wave.

"That's your friend. I met him in Germany, but I don't remember his name."

"His name is Keon, but everyone calls him Edge."

"He is a good friend to you."

"He's my best mate. Has been so since our days at Sandhurst."

"Was he there?"

Pia's voice was soft, and I knew she didn't mean at the Royal Military Academy. "Yes, he was."

"It must have been so difficult for him."

She was right, and it was something I didn't acknowledge often enough. My head was filled to capacity with how awful it had been for me, and I rarely thought about the pain of others. Every so often, I'd see the light, but most of the time, I was mired down in my own darkness.

"He feels guilty. It's common among those who serve. Most call it survivor's guilt. In this case, I survived, but there were others there that day who did not."

Pia stopped dancing and took a step back. "Excuse me…I'm sorry." She rushed away, and I followed.

"Let her go," said Edge as I was about to blow by him. "Give her a minute. She'll be back."

I shrugged off the hand he'd put on my arm. "How do you know?"

"I just do." A waiter walked past us with a tray of champagne. Edge grabbed two glasses and handed one to me. "Welcome back, ya wanker."

"Thanks." We toasted.

"Z Alexander has been asking about you."

"Why would the head of SIS ask about me?"

"Maybe because you were trained to eventually work for him."

"Not going to happen."

Edge took my glass and set it and his on a nearby table. "Let's find a real drink, yes?"

I led him over to the bar, where we both ordered an Irish and a pint.

"There's a job at MI5 when you're ready."

"It isn't something I ever see myself capable of doing."

"Capable? Of course you're capable."

I pushed the shot glass across the bar, and the man behind it poured me another. "Drop it, Edge. I'm not interested."

He stared at me with an open mouth. "You're twenty-six years old, and it's the only thing you've been trained to do. What do you plan to do instead?"

"I said to drop it."

He lowered his voice and leaned into me. "I'm not going to bloody drop it, Grind. Tell me what the fuck you plan to do."

"I don't know yet."

"Then come in. At least talk to Z."

There were reasons I couldn't do that. My sister knew it, and I got the impression Pia might too. No matter what the level of my injuries was, or my pain, I couldn't function in an environment where having my wits about me at every conceivable moment was required.

"I'm not going to let this go, Grind."

I saw Pia walk back into the ballroom. She looked over at me and then scanned the crowd. When she saw Lily and Wills, she approached them.

"At least for tonight. Please."

He walked away without answering, and I knew he would do as I asked and let it be. Tomorrow, though, would be an entirely different story.

I made my rounds, saying hello to my parents' friends, meeting those of Lily and Wills, accepting the concern of those privy to my struggles with as much grace as I could muster.

Apart from Pia, there wasn't anyone here I had any interest in talking to.

When I approached, her back was to me. I scowled at Lily in warning, and she pretended not to see me. If my sister got Pia involved in something that wasn't her business in the first place, she'd face my wrath.

"What do you say we get out of here for a bit?" I whispered into Pia's ear.

When she looked over her shoulder, her lips were close enough that I could kiss them. Instead, I backed away.

"We need to talk, Pia," I said when my sister left us alone.

She turned toward me. "I'm sorry for the way I left. It just…I can't…"

I reached up and cupped her cheek with my palm when her eyes filled with tears. "I understand."

"It isn't pity, Mylos."

"Somewhere inside me, I think I know that. It's the reason I want us to talk."

"Will we be coming back to the party?"

"That's up to you."

"Let me say goodbye to your parents, Lily, and her husband."

"Let's do it together." I took her hand in mine.

While they expressed disappointment, my family members also appeared somewhat relieved. Perhaps they sensed—like deep inside, I did—that spending time alone with Pia would be good for me.

When we exited the ballroom, the first thing I did was loosen my tie, take it off, and slip it into my jacket pocket.

"Where are we going?" Pia asked when I stopped short in the middle of the lobby.

I hadn't gotten that far. I really didn't want to go back to my parents' place, and we were overdressed to go to a restaurant.

"Come, Mylos," she said, leading me to the bank of lifts.

"Pia, I wasn't suggesting—"

"I'll change out of this dress, and we can decide from there."

When I'd gone to her room earlier, I saw through the open door that she had a suite. That was probably the only reason she was inviting me up. Or maybe when we got there, she'd ask me to wait for her in the hallway.

I reached into my pocket and found the two things that would settle my overwhelming anxiety. The first was her stone. The second was the bottle of pills my sister had been gracious enough to leave me. *The bint*.

"Mi scusi," Pia said once we were in the suite.

She opened a door, went into the bedroom, and closed it behind her. I walked over to the bar area, filled a glass with water, and got out my bottle of pills. After shaking three into my hand, I put them in my mouth and swallowed. I closed my eyes, knowing that soon the calm I craved would wash over me. When I turned around, Pia was standing in the doorway, wearing a jumper and a pair of joggers.

Her eyes were scrunched as she studied me.

"Lily told you her concern."

She nodded. "She's worried about you."

"Needlessly."

She walked closer. "You can lie to her, you can even lie to me, but you cannot lie to yourself, Mylos."

"I should go."

She shrugged. "Perhaps you should."

I hated she wasn't at least trying to stop me.

"Or you can stay, but if you do, you'll have to tell me the truth."

"What's your plan, Pia? Interrogation? Don't forget my training."

She shook her head. *"Stronzo."* She sat on the arm of the sofa and folded her arms. "You said you wanted to talk. What about, Mylos? The weather? Our vineyard performance? Or maybe you wanted to ask about *my* life?"

"How is your life, Pia?"

"It isn't good." She shifted, and instead of sitting on the arm, she sat on the sofa's cushion.

I walked closer so I could see her face. "Why not?"

"Many things," she murmured, not looking at me.

"Tell me about them."

"Because you care?"

"Of course I do. I'll always care about you, Pia."

She didn't say anything for several seconds, as though she was weighing whether she believed me.

"I am twenty-six years old. Do you know what my life is like?"

I shook my head when she turned to face me.

"I get up in the morning, and the first thing I do is check on my mother. Why? Because I live with her. Why else? Because she's getting older and she's all alone." She shook her head. "And then I go down to the winery. If Georgio, the head winemaker, is there, he argues with me. It doesn't matter what about. The subject changes daily, but the underlying theme is that I am a terrible manager."

"I'm sure he's wrong."

She leveled her gaze on me. "Is he?"

"To be honest, I don't know."

"He's approached me about selling."

"Selling what? Valentini? Is that even a possibility?"

She sighed. *"Sì."*

"Is there a reason you need to sell?"

"Not now, but if things don't get better soon, there might be."

I sat beside her. "Is there anyone in your family who can help?"

She nodded. "My cousin Mateo has offered."

"Why don't you take him up on it?"

"He won't let me pay him."

I raised a brow and then wished I hadn't. Her finances weren't any of my business.

"He and Lucia…do you remember Lucia?"

"Vaguely. All I really remember is you."

She smiled and her cheeks turned pink.

"Lucia came to me after my papà was injured and told me I needed to allow people to help me." She looked into my eyes and then away. "I'm not good at that."

"So, Mateo?"

"Right. He and Lucia have been seeing each other for a couple of years. Since I was a young girl, I thought one day my father would want him to take over Valentini. He's the second son of my father's sister, so he will not inherit his family's estate. But that was before I knew about Estancia Valentini's curse."

"Curse?"

"It's a long story, but the point is, it would not be advisable for me to go against her wishes and deny my inheritance."

"But you can sell? No curses to worry about then?"

Her eyes opened wide. "I hadn't thought of that." She shuddered. "Where was I?"

"Mateo. What does he think about Georgio's suggestion that you sell?"

"I haven't discussed it with him."

"It might be beneficial to get his input."

She nodded and rolled her shoulders. "I shouldn't complain. Compared to what you've been through—"

I put my hand on her arm. "Please."

"I'm sure Valentini will be fine."

"Talk to me, Pia," I urged again. "Tell me what you're going through."

Her shoulders rose and fell with the deep breath she took and then let out slowly. "The equipment we have is getting older. We've been plagued by failures, among other things. We're not in a position to invest a lot of money to make updates, but then almost as much ends up going into repairs."

For the first time since she arrived this afternoon, I noticed how tired she looked. There was no spark in her eyes as she spoke about something I knew she loved.

"Are you giving up?"

"Giving up? No. Considering the offer Georgio brought to me? Perhaps."

How could a winemaker afford to buy her out? "Where is he getting his capital?"

"Georgio wouldn't buy Valentini. His investors would."

"Where would you go?"

"I don't know."

"This is more than a winery, Pia. This is your birthright."

"Sì," she said again. "Perhaps I don't deserve it."

I hoped she was exaggerating, but I wouldn't assume anything at this point. "If you had an influx of cash, would you be able to recover?"

Pia leaned back and closed her eyes. "Maybe. I'm not certain." She took a deep breath and let it out slowly.

"Come here," I said, pulling her into my arms when I saw a tear run down her face.

She rested her cheek against my heart. "It's one thing after another, Mylos. I'm exhausted from it. What made me think I could do this?"

She turned in my arms so her body was pressed against mine and then looked up at me. I knew what her eyes were asking: she wanted comfort, but I couldn't give it to her. Not this way.

When she leaned up and brought her mouth to mine, I turned my head. When she rested her hand on my trousers, I moved it away. When she tried to stand, I held her in my arms. I hated rejecting her, but I had no choice. "I'm sorry. It isn't you, Pia."

She jerked out of my arms and turned her back to me.

I spun her around and looked into her eyes. "It isn't you," I repeated, pulling her body into mine. Having her this close, made me so hard it hurt. It had been true when I held her in my arms as we danced. It was true now. I couldn't stop my body's reaction to her.

When she stiffened, I released her. She rushed into the bedroom and closed the door.

I should leave. Accept this for what it was—the end for Pia and me. The odds were against us. They always had been. Our attraction was undeniable, but I wasn't the same man I had been, nor would I ever be again.

It would be best for both of us if I left now and never looked back.

I had my hand on the door, ready to walk out, when I heard her soft sobs. I remembered earlier when she commented on Edge and how hard what had happened to me must have been on him. It occurred to me that I spent so much time thinking about myself, I didn't consider the pain of others. Wasn't that what I was doing now? Pia, already in a vulnerable state, had reached out to me, and I rejected her because of my own fear. I'd even said the words myself. *It isn't you, Pia.*

Instead of leaving, I walked over and checked the handle; the door to the bedroom wasn't locked, so I went inside. I could see Pia's fragile form on the bed. I joined her and tried to pull her toward me, but she resisted. Instead, I shifted closer and wrapped my body around hers.

I moved her hair from her neck and kissed her soft skin. I trailed my lips down and heard her whimper, "Don't pity me, Mylos."

"I would never. There's nothing to pity. You're the strongest, most courageous woman I know." Her body shook and I held on tight.

"I'm sorry," I murmured as my lips scattered kisses on her shoulder.

"Why are you sorry? You did nothing."

That was exactly right. I'd done nothing. Nothing for anyone but myself. "I want to help you."

"There isn't anything you can do," she said with a heavy sigh.

There was, but there'd be time for us to talk about that later.

"Let me take care of you, Pia. Right here, right now. Let me hold you."

"Why didn't you leave?"

"Something you said earlier made me realize how selfish I am."

"Mylos?"

I kissed the side of her face. "Yes?"

"Is it because…you can't?"

I kissed the soft curve of her neck. "Not in the way you mean."

She turned in my arms. "In another way? Is it the pain?"

It was difficult to speak the things that ran through my mind, especially to Pia. "It is the pain. Sometimes."

I tensed when I felt her unfastening the buttons on my shirt.

"When it isn't the pain, what is it?"

When her hands touched my bare skin, my already aching erection pressed against my trousers.

She leaned forward and kissed the indentation at the bottom of my sternum. When her lips trailed farther down my body, I drew her back up.

"I want to see."

"Pia…"

"Let me see, Mylos."

I stopped her hand when she started to unfasten my trousers. "I can't."

Her eyes bored into mine. "Why not? Have you not seen? Do you not look at yourself every day?"

"It's different and you know it."

She sat up so quickly, I was startled until I realized she was pulling the jumper over her head. When she unfastened her bra and freed her breasts, I was scream- ing inside for her to stop, but my brain refused to say the words out loud. Just to see her naked body would be enough. It would have to be enough.

Pia didn't stop. Next, she slid her joggers down and off her legs. The only thing she wore was a tiny red lace thong. She stretched out on her side in front of me, took one of my hands, and put it on her bare breast.

"Feel me, Mylos. Touch me." I couldn't resist. I had to have a taste of her. I lowered my mouth to her breast and swirled my tongue around her hardened nipple. I could hear her heart pounding, or maybe it was my own. I licked my way down her abdomen and moved the lace of her thong out of my way.

I shifted to kneel between her legs and breathed in the scent of her. Her hips gyrated on the bed. I stilled her with my fingers, then lowered my mouth.

"Wait."

I looked up at her.

"Mylos, I need you."

"I'm right here, sweetheart."

"No." She shook her head. "I won't come until you are inside me. You, Mylos."

I dropped my head on her tummy. "Don't do this. Please don't do this."

She scooted back so she was sitting up.

When I rolled to my back and looked up at the ceiling, Pia straddled me. She finished unfastening the buttons on my shirt and slowly kissed her way from my lips down to my abdomen.

"Let me love you, Mylos. Trust me to love you."

I knew what her words meant and, more importantly, what they didn't. She wasn't talking about our hearts; she was talking about her body and mine.

I slowly nodded my head—once. Just as slowly, Pia unfastened my trousers and eased them from my hips. When I tried to help, she pushed my hands away. "Let me love you, Mylos," she repeated.

The way her eyes traveled the length of my body was as though every inch of my skin looked the same. I almost cried out with the anxiety of what she was putting me through, but was it warranted? Was she doing anything beyond "loving" me?

As she made her way back up my body, she stopped and licked the length of my shaft, and with that, I almost ejaculated. But she quickly moved, straddling me.

She raised her hips and positioned my cock at the source of her wetness. Slowly, so slowly I was in agony, she lowered herself until I was buried as deep inside her as I could get. Pia placed her hands on my torso and looked at me.

"You cannot deny how right this is, Mylos. There has been no one—there will be no one—whose body fits more perfectly with mine." When she began to move, I grasped her hips with my hands, setting our rhythm.

Too soon, I felt myself losing control. My eyes met hers, and in them, I saw her heat had risen to mine. "Don't stop," she begged.

The pace of our combined movement increased until I knew I couldn't hold off any longer.

"Now, Pia, now!"

I closed my eyes then, so I could focus solely on how unbelievably perfect she felt.

With the movement of a cat, she stretched her body the length of mine, her skin touching mine. No one, other than the doctors and Carson, had touched the left side of my body since I was taken to the burn unit in Germany, and yet, the tingling, restless feelings I anticipated didn't materialize. I wasn't anxious to move away from her, or even cover myself.

Within what felt like mere minutes, Pia began to make her way back down my body. My cock sprung to life as she kissed my torso, under my belly button, but then instead of continuing where I expected her to, she shifted. Her tongue and lips began to love the length of my burn. Slowly, languidly, she studied the changes in my body since the last time we were skin to skin.

I rested my head against the pillow, never dreaming I would lie naked with anyone again. Not ever. Yet Pia made me feel like this was the most natural, perfect thing in the world.

Tears ran down my cheeks. "Thank you," I whispered. Did she know that what I was thanking her for was showing me, proving to me, I was a whole man? A man who, truly, had a life worth living.

We spent the next three days in her hotel room, shutting out the rest of the world. The only human interaction we had was with the hotel staff who delivered sustenance by way of room service.

When Pia and I bathed together that first night, I showed her how to clean the areas that were still healing. Afterward, we applied the lotions and salves that would keep my skin properly moisturized.

After, each time we emerged from a bath or shower, she insisted I allow her to be the one to care for me. There were times I was so emotionally overwhelmed I couldn't hold back my tears.

In the same way she cared for the outside of my body, she nurtured the inside with the softness of her words, her hands, her lips. I truly had no idea it was possible to feel as cared for as I did. As Pia made me feel.

The idea that our time together would soon come to an end, filled me with sadness.

We heard a knock. I wrapped myself in one of the robes the hotel supplied and padded to the door in anticipation of dinner's arrival.

Instead of room service, my sister stood on the other side. "I'm sorry to interrupt," she said, thrusting my medicine pack at me. "Forgive me, Miles."

"Wait," I said when she began to walk away. I opened the pack, removed a single bottle, zipped it closed, and handed it back to her. There weren't many pills in the bottle I chose. I'd picked it intentionally. "I'll be in touch."

Lily nodded. "If you need anything…"

I pulled her into my arms and hugged her. "Thank you, Lil."

"I love you, Miles."

I nodded and watched as she walked to the lift without looking back. I closed the door and turned to find Pia standing a few feet from me.

"I'm sorry," she said.

"For?"

"Not realizing you would need more." Her gaze was on the bottle of pills in my hand.

"I don't want to need more, Pia."

She stepped closer and put her arms around me. "Tell me what I can do, Mylos."

I led her over to the sofa and sat beside her. "I'm going to contact Carson and see if he can arrange for me to get into a treatment program." With wide eyes, she hung on my every word. "It will need to be at an in-patient facility."

"Okay."

"I know you need to get back to Valentini, but if there is any way you could stay until I've spoken with Carson…"

"I will stay, Mylos. As long as you need me to."

The next morning, Pia and I hired a car from the hotel. We drove together to the Wellington Rehabilitation Centre, where Carson stood outside, waiting.

"Thank you, Pia," I said before kissing her, long and hard. "You gave me my life back."

"Mylos, I—"

I kissed away her words. "I'll see you soon?"

"*Sì*. Soon."

12

Grinder
Two Years Later
London, England

"You're better suited staying with MI5," said Z Alexander. As disappointed as I was not to be promoted to a position in Military Intelligence Section 6, I wouldn't complain. Not to Z, not to anyone. I was lucky to work here at all. SIS had taken a big chance on me eighteen months ago when I finished rehab, and I appreciated the opportunity.

"Thank you, sir," I said when Z picked up a file on his desk and began thumbing through it. When he nodded, I stood and walked out.

"Well?" asked Edge, waiting for me.

"Remaining with MI5."

"I'm staying put too."

I raised a brow and studied him. "Why?"

"Z's decision, mate."

"That's bloody bullshit." I slammed past him. Instead of waiting for the lift, I took the stairs. When

I got to street level, Edge was waiting for me. "I don't need a fucking nursemaid," I seethed.

"Did it occur to you that this wasn't my choice?"

"Sod off." What I wanted more than anything was a pint, but since Edge would just follow me, I stalked in the direction of my flat. As I expected, he remained by my side the entire way.

When we arrived at my building, he followed me upstairs. Had I really expected him to do differently? I handed him a beer and sat down.

"I know you're brassed off, but look at it this way, our careers have always followed the same path. How is this any different than both of us being accepted to Monckton, or getting the same intel assignment?"

"You could do better," I muttered, watching as he took a long drink.

"Now you can sod off."

Most of the MI5 missions were cooperative assignments with MI6. Domestic terrorism was on the rise, necessitating a combined effort with the international section.

We were in our morning briefing with one of the senior MI6 agents, Rile, when Z Alexander stepped into the room. "Wilder, repeat what you've just told me." He put the call on speaker so we could all hear.

"There are reports coming in that there have been five simultaneous explosions in the underground. Stepping Square, Kensington Street, Lawrence Road, Chancery, and Hampstead stations. Multiple fatalities."

Z nodded at the collective group, and we began mobilizing into predetermined teams. MI5 would lead the action since the attacks occurred within the UK. Additional resources would be arriving; our number-one priority would be to get bomb squads out to as many stations as we could, as quickly as possible. That there would be more explosions, more fatalities, was an imminent threat.

"You okay?" asked Edge as we donned tactical gear.

I looked behind us to see if anyone else was in earshot. "I don't know."

My expectation was that I would "enter a zone" and do what needed to be done. However, if another explosion occurred within range, I honestly couldn't predict what my reaction would be. There wasn't another living soul I'd admit that to. Edge knew that, and I trusted him.

"Ready?" he asked.

I nodded and followed him out the door.

Each team was sent to a different station. I went to Arnos Grove; Edge, to Warren. As I rode in the transport vehicle, thoughts raced through my mind. I put my hands on my head, feeling a migraine coming on like those I suffered when the memories of the explosion became unbearable.

This was the true test of whether I was capable of performing the duties for which I'd vowed. If I failed, I doubted I'd be able to live with myself.

I reached into my pocket and rubbed the stone that had become my talisman. It had been in my right trouser pocket the day I came as close to dying as a man ever should. Given the men triaging me had to cut the clothing from my body, the fact that the stone had been recovered was a testament to its power.

I closed my eyes, allowing myself to picture Pia the last time we were together. She'd given me a gift, and no matter whether we were ever able to find our way back to each other, I'd remain eternally grateful to her for bringing me back into the light.

The transport pulled up to the Arnos Grove station, and our team exited the vehicle. Something was about to go down here; I could feel it in my bones.

As Rile directed the team to unload the bomb dogs, officially known as explosive detection canines, I turned in a slow circle, surveying the scene and getting a read on my surroundings.

A double-decker bus full of tourists was headed in our direction. So far, the bombings had been in the underground, not out on the street, but there was just something nagging at me. I spun around and whistled at Rile, who was headed down into the tube.

"Hold up!" I shouted, pointing at the bus.

He nodded and called after another team member. They were headed my way when we heard it. An explosion tore the roof off the double-decker, sending debris flying through the air. In horror, I ran toward the scene. Before I could see well enough to start pulling out victims, the top level of the bus collapsed into the bottom.

This was it. The first test of the kind of man I was. There were people inside that bus, bodies on fire the same as mine had been.

Without further hesitation, I raced in and began pulling the victims, both dead and alive, from the rubble.

Beside me were the team I'd arrived here with along with countless other civilian volunteers.

At final count, sixty-three people died in the bus explosion, including some who were hit by flying debris. The explosive device had gone off on the rear of the top level. The majority of casualties had been seated in that area and had suffered burns ranging from seventy to ninety percent of their body.

Hours later, the bomb dogs had found ten more undetonated devices in a van parked one block from Arnos Grove.

The casualty count from the tube explosions hadn't yet been verified, given the number of locations and the difficulty in body recovery. Injury counts were in the thousands.

"Three weeks mandatory leave," Z said when he called me into his office after the final briefing on the terrorist attacks.

"Unnecessary," I countered. In fact, that Z thought I needed it, really brassed me off. I'd done my duty without hesitation, even in the face of something that might've cut me off at my knees.

He looked up at me and scrunched his eyes. "Did you not hear the word *mandatory*?"

"Is anyone else on forced leave?"

Z stood and rested both of his hands on the desk in front of him. "Yes."

I suppose he was waiting for me to challenge him, but I didn't.

"Whether you were injured during a previous mission or not, the same edict would've come down. This is not personal. Be on your way, then, before I extend it to four weeks."

"Yes, sir."

I left his office and went to mine. I didn't keep much here; I was rarely at Vauxhall Cross. I was about to walk out when Rile, the MI6 agent who had been with me at Arnos Grove, caught up with me.

"Forced leave?" I asked.

"Mandatory," he growled in an accent that was as much Spanish as it was English. I knew his background. Cortez "Rile" DeLéon's father, Carlos DeLéon, Duke of Soria, was the youngest brother of King Felipe VI of Spain. His mother was second cousin to Elizabeth II, Queen of the United Kingdom. With dual citizenship and connectivity to royalty, Rile had become an early asset to SIS.

With that kind of lineage, it was impossible to say whether his affectations were that, or just who he was.

"Fancy a pint?" he said, motioning to the pub across from Vauxhall Cross.

"I'll have one."

When we walked in, Edge was already seated at one of the tables. He waved us over.

"Go ahead," said Rile, indicating he'd place our order.

"Is this a coincidence?" I asked as I sat on the other side of the table.

"Hardly," he answered, laughing.

"What's it about, then?"

Rile sat down and set a glass in front of me and handed the other to Edge.

"Gentlemen," he said. "Thank you for joining me."

I raised an eyebrow at Edge, and we both laughed. Rile continued as though we hadn't.

"I'm leaving MI6."

I looked at Edge a second time, and he shrugged.

"I'd like you both to come with me."

"Where are you going, mate?" Edge asked.

Rile raised a brow, but not in humor.

"Right," said Edge. "But seriously. Where?"

"I'm starting my own firm. Private security and intelligence. I'm looking for partners."

I leaned back, suddenly uncomfortable with the direction of this conversation. "I can't speak for Edge, but why me?"

Rile brushed his bottom lip with his index finger. "I'm curious why you would question it."

"Some say I'm more of a liability than an asset."

Rile nodded. "They weren't at Arnos Grove."

"Is Lennox aware you're approaching us?"

Lennox, known by those in SIS as Lynx, was Keon's older brother. Like Rile, he was a senior agent in MI6.

Rile nodded his head slowly. He appeared amused. "He is aware."

"What about Z?"

"As it so happens, he indicated he would be anxious to work with a firm such as ours."

"Did he, now?"

I didn't know Rile well enough to have much of an opinion of him, but it seemed as though Edge didn't like him. Either that, or he was in a particularly argumentative mood tonight. Which, of late, had been happening on a more frequent basis.

"I've another question."

I considered kicking Edge under the table. I didn't understand why he was being so combative. If this was something he didn't want to do, wouldn't it be easier to simply decline Rile's offer?

He motioned for Edge to go on.

"What's the buy-in?"

Rile smiled. Not grinned or smirked—smiled. "Five mil."

"Euros?"

"Pounds sterling."

It was a hefty amount, but Rile wouldn't have approached either of us if he didn't already know we had it.

"What's the split?" Edge asked.

"Equal. Among four."

"Who's the fourth?" I asked.

"Decker Ashford."

I was tempted, but held it in. Edge, on the other hand, laughed out loud. "Good bloody luck. No way in hell Ashford will sign on."

I watched Rile's reaction. He clearly knew something neither Edge nor I did. If I were a betting man, I'd lay odds Ashford had already agreed.

Most in the intelligence world knew of the American man by reputation alone. There were rumors that when Z Alexander married a woman from Texas and settled in the States, he adopted Ashford when he was a teen. Seeing something in the boy, Z made arrangements for him to study with the master of all masters of intelligence technology—Burns Butler. It was said that even Burns considered Decker to be more accomplished in the field.

There were also rumors that governments, including the UK and the US, had offered Ashford ungodly sums of money to come work for them, and he'd consistently refused. Even Burns' son, Kade, who was also a partner in a private intelligence firm, had attempted to recruit Decker. If Rile was so confident he'd be successful where so many others had not, I could only assume he had something on the guy. Something big.

"I'm in, as long as both Ashford and Grinder are."

Rile brushed his bottom lip with his finger like he had earlier. It was a tell, but I hadn't figured out exactly what for yet.

"You're either in or you're out. There are no ifs."

Edge nodded. "Did Lennox turn you down?"

"Why would you ask?"

"I'm assuming you went to him first."

Rile shook his head slowly. His expression changed to one of disappointment.

"I'm in." I blurted the words almost as a man possessed. Seconds ago, I was leaning toward a polite decline.

Edge's eyes opened wide. "You are?"

I nodded.

"Bloody hell. Then, I am too."

For the second time, Rile smiled.

"What are we calling ourselves?" I asked.

"The Invincible Intelligence and Security Group."

Edge looked from Rile to me and back again. "You can't be serious?"

For a third time, Rile smiled, confirming he was serious, indeed.

13

Pia
Val d'Orcia, Italy

"You're going to have to make some kind of decision, Pia," said Georgio. I lost count of how many times we'd had this conversation. "We don't have the money we need to invest in new equipment, and without it, we're crippled. The longer you wait, the less you'll be able to get for it."

I knew Georgio was right. I just couldn't bear the thought of selling Valentini. "There are other things I'm working on. Things that can bring in additional income."

"Like what?"

"It isn't to do with the winery."

The door opened then, and Lucia walked in. "Am I interrupting?"

Before I could answer, Georgio stood and stalked out.

"What was that about?"

I didn't want to burden Lucia, but I needed someone to talk to. "He wants me to sell."

"Georgio wants you to sell? What business is it of his?"

"Things aren't going well, Lucia."

"I'm sure Mateo would be more than happy to help you. He's offered many times."

"I thought you said he had a new job?"

"He does, but if he knew you were struggling this much, I'm sure he could work something out."

"I appreciate that, Lucia, but this is my problem to solve." As hard as it would be, I'd reached the point where I'd have to tell my mother how bad things had gotten.

"I'm sorry, Pia." She looked out the window for a minute and then back at me. "What about Mylos? What happened when you saw him in London? You never really said."

While Mylos and I didn't make each other any promises, the fact that I'd heard so little from him after he entered rehab, hurt. I'd written a couple of letters, got perfunctory responses, and then gave up. I hoped I'd hear more from him, but I hadn't.

"There isn't anything he can do, Lucia."

"Maybe not, but maybe you could go and visit him again. You know, just to get your mind off things."

I knew my friend was trying to help, but she was only making me feel worse. "That's a good idea. I'll think about it."

The next morning, I heard an alert that someone was at the front gate as I exited the shower. The winery wasn't open yet, so other than workers, who would have the code, no one should be entering Valentini at this hour. Whoever it was, I was sure would realize we weren't open yet and leave.

I finished drying myself and getting dressed and was about to go to the kitchen when I heard a knock at the front door.

My mother, a night owl, wouldn't be up this early, so I padded my way downstairs, puzzled by why neither Nonna Bella nor Nonna Carina had come to see who was knocking. I looked out the window, surprised to see Paolo.

"What are you doing here?" He called from time to time to check to see how I was doing, but I hadn't seen him since we ran into each other at the hotel in London.

"*Buongiorno,* Pia." He winked.

I smiled and lowered my eyes. "*Buongiorno,* Paolo."

"Can I come in?"

"Of course." I stepped aside and closed the door behind him. "Why are you here?"

"I wanted you to know that Donnatella and I never married."

My eyes scrunched. "You woke up and decided that was important information to share with me at nine in the morning? In person, no less?"

He rubbed the back of his neck. "I've wanted to see you…" I waited, but he didn't continue. What's more, he appeared pained.

I haven't had any coffee yet and could really use a cup. *"Vuoi un caffè?"*

"Sì. Grazie."

I went into the kitchen, surprised not to find Nonna Bella making breakfast. Instead, it looked as though she hadn't been in yet.

I made us each a coffee, put some fruit on a plate, and met Paolo out on the *terrazza*.

"Grazie," he said a second time.

"Why are you here, Paolo?" I asked for the third time.

"Ever since that night…seeing you in London…I told you then that I missed you."

I took a sip of coffee and then a bite of strawberry. "When I saw you with…"

"Donnatella."

"Right. I thought you'd moved on."

He leaned forward, covered my hand with his, and looked into my eyes. "I don't want to move on. I want you, Pia. We could be good together if you'd just give us a chance."

I moved my hand away, scooted my chair back, stood, and walked over to the railing. "Why me?"

"What do you mean?"

"There are hundreds of other women in Tuscany more interesting than I am."

He walked over and grasped my hand with his. "You've never realized how alluring you are, Pia. There is no other woman in all of Italy I'd rather spend time with than you."

I laughed. "Sorry if this offends you, Paolo, but I cannot believe that."

"Give me a chance to prove it to you."

Was I being foolish? Paolo had been good to me. He'd worked hard at Valentini, and I knew he'd been disappointed when I told him I was ready to take over after I finished college. He'd asked then if I would consider a relationship with him, and I'd said I wasn't ready to think about dating anyone. He'd accepted my rejection gracefully, and as I'd said, when I saw him in London, I thought he'd moved on.

"Go out to dinner with me. Spend time with me. Let's get to know each other again."

"I'm very busy…"

"Dinner, Pia. Let's start there. If by the end of our meal, I've bored you too much, you can decline another date with me."

Why did it feel like if I agreed, I'd be cheating on Mylos? We'd never been together as a couple nor could we be. Our lives were full, and they were led in two different places.

He'd never asked for more than the brief interludes we shared, nor had I. I was twenty-six years old, and like Paolo said, I did little other than work. Why not accept his offer?

"Okay. Dinner."

Paolo smiled. "I'll pick you up tomorrow night at seven. We'll go into the village."

I took our cups and dishes into the kitchen after he left. Georgio was there, looking as though he'd been waiting for me.

"Hi," I said, not liking the look on his face.

"Hey. I have some bad news."

I set the things I carried in on the counter and walked closer to him. "What's wrong, Georgio?"

"It's Nonna Bella…"

I covered my mouth when his eyes filled with tears. "What's happened?"

"She'll be okay, but she had a heart attack last night."

"She did? How do I not already know this?"

"I didn't want to bother your family—"

"Bother our family? You are our family, Georgio. Both you and Nonna Bella. Tell me what happened!"

"She called me last night and said she wasn't feeling well. When I arrived, her color didn't look good and she was having a hard time breathing. I rushed her to the emergency room, and they confirmed she'd had a heart attack."

"When was this?"

He ran his hands through his hair. "Around nine."

Georgio had moved off the estate shortly after he was promoted to winemaker. His place in the village was at least twenty minutes away. "Why didn't she tell one of us? Call one of us? Why didn't you?"

"I already told you."

I nodded. His mother had had a heart attack. The last thing Georgio needed was for me to berate him or her for not letting us know she needed help.

"Tell me what I can do."

He raised his head as if my words surprised him. "It will be quite a while before she's able to come back to work. If ever."

"Okay."

"I'd like to ask that you consider letting her live here until I find another place for her."

"No."

"No? Jesus, Pia—"

"No, you will not find another place for her. She will stay in the home she's always known, for as long as she'd like. She can stay there forever."

"But…"

I waited, but he didn't continue. "But what, Georgio?"

"I've just told you. She might not be able to come back to work—"

"I don't care about that. I mean, I care very much about Nonna Bella, but if she can't come back to work, it makes no difference. We're not going to ask her to leave her home. Additionally, she'll continue to draw the same salary."

His eyes opened wide. "For how long?"

"Forever."

"You can't afford to do that. This place is already in trouble."

Georgio was upset about his mother. I was too. He was stressed, tired, and uncertain about the future. I got all that. "Let me worry about Valentini. You worry about your mother."

I saw the struggle from within him. He was a proud man, but in this case, he needed to accept what I was telling him. He had no choice. Even if he disagreed, it didn't matter. I would still do everything I could for Nonna Bella. It saddened me to think she felt as though she couldn't call upon me if she was feeling poorly. I could've gotten to her in a matter of minutes.

"Thank you," I heard Georgio say as he turned to walk out.

"May I see her?"

He turned around as though my question surprised him. "Of course." I watched him walk away.

A few minutes after I started washing the dishes Paolo and I had used, Georgio came back.

"Do you think you'll look for another cook?"

I shrugged. "I wouldn't want Nonna Bella to think we're anxious to replace her."

He nodded. "I might have another solution."

"Tell me."

"My cousin, Gabriella, might be able to help out, at least for a while."

Gabriella? This was the first I'd heard of Georgio having a cousin, but considering his mother didn't trust us to call when she didn't feel well, maybe I didn't know their family as well as I always thought I did.

Later that afternoon, I went to the hospital to visit her only to find she was no longer there. I tried to call Georgio, but my call went straight to voicemail. When I returned to Valentini, I stopped by her cottage, but no one answered the door.

I needed to get back to the winery, but I needed to talk with my mamma more. I found her resting in bed. For several weeks, my mother had been ill. Our cook's heart attack only made me worry about her more.

"How is Nonna Bella doing?" she asked.

"She wasn't there."

She lowered the book she'd been reading. "What do you mean?"

"Exactly that. The hospital said they didn't have a patient by the name of Isabella Rossi."

"Odd."

"Georgio said his cousin, Gabriella, could fill in temporarily, longer if necessary."

"It's your decision, Pia."

"Did you know he had a cousin?"

"No, but I do know Nonna Bella has a sister who lives in the village. Maybe it's her daughter."

"Mamma, doesn't it bother you that we know so little of their family?"

She shook her head. "It isn't our business, Pia."

I walked to the winery, feeling as though my universe had tilted. Things I'd always believed would never change, were, faster than I could keep up. Perhaps this was what growing up felt like. The things that had always been, weren't any longer, and I, like everyone else, was expected to adapt.

For the next several weeks, Paolo and I saw each other often. It was over an hour's drive from his family's estate in Chianti to Valentini, but he never complained. At least twice a week, he'd come and take me to dinner. Some days he'd arrive earlier and try to coax me into leaving work. It was rare that I could, but he remained good-natured about it.

He offered his help, and when I declined, he didn't push.

I found myself looking forward to spending time with him, but my attraction to him paled whenever I thought of Mylos.

I received a few more letters from him. When each arrived, I felt happier than I did whenever Paolo showed up to take me out. There were times I thought about telling him we couldn't see each other anymore, but other than a few chaste goodnight kisses, we weren't much more than friends anyway.

During the harvest, I had far less time to spend with Paolo, and he too was needed in Chianti. At the end of a particularly busy week, he walked into the winery, surprising me.

"There she is," he said, bringing me a bouquet of flowers. I realized then that he'd left more than one message and I'd never returned his calls.

"Thank you, and I'm sorry. It's been so—"

"Busy." He smiled. "I understand. It's the nature of the wine business. But, Pia, you're running yourself into the ground. Do you realize we haven't spoken for almost three weeks?"

Had it been that long?

He took a step forward and cupped my cheek. "You can't do this alone, and you know it. Why can't you let go of your pride and let me help you?"

Perhaps it was due to how tired I was, but I wondered if Paolo would dare say the same thing to a man.

"I'm perfectly capable of running Valentini, Paolo."

"Are you, Pia? Truly?"

"What do you mean?"

"It isn't a secret that your sales are down since I left and you took over."

I bristled. "Everyone's are."

"Not everyone's."

After a few years of high yields, production was up, and as a result, there was less demand. Additionally, with older estates like ours being purchased by corporations who could afford to invest a great deal of money into both equipment and marketing, it was harder for the ones that remained family-owned to compete.

"I have some other things in the works to offset our decline in sales." The minute I uttered the words, I wished I hadn't.

"You do? I'd love to hear about them."

Paolo was as charming and gracious as always, and there was no good reason for me not to tell him. Except I didn't. "I'll let you know more as they develop."

He leaned forward and kissed me. "Beautiful, sweet, brave Pia. Always determined to do things on your own. When will you learn you can ask for help?"

He sounded like Lucia, but with less sincerity. "Perhaps when I need it."

"What do you say we go into the village for dinner?"

"Thank you, Paolo, but no. If you'd called first, I would've told you I was too busy."

"I did call. Multiple times."

"I'm sorry, the answer is still no."

I could see his body tensing, but the smile remained on his face nonetheless. I knew he was angry, but he was fighting hard to control it. Why?

"I'm leaving in a few days on a sales trip, first to the UK and then to America. That was one of the reasons I've been calling. I'm offering to represent Valentini along with our winery."

Interesting. I couldn't be the only person in the region who'd come up with the idea to boost sales by increasing exports. However, I wouldn't trust anyone to represent Valentini on my behalf—even Paolo.

"When are you leaving?"

"As I said, in a few days. Once the harvest has wound down."

"Instead of representing Valentini, why don't you take me with you? I can't go to America, but I could go to the UK."

I could tell by the look on his face he was stunned.

"Of course…sure…that would be wonderful," he stammered. When he reached out and hugged me, my body stiffened. "Pia?"

"I'm sorry, Paolo. As you said, I've been working so much. I'm just exhausted."

He kissed my forehead and looked into my eyes. "We'll have some time to relax during our travels. I'm so pleased you're coming with me."

"I said I could go to the UK, Paolo. I can't afford to be away very long."

After he left, I wondered if he'd heard me.

14

Grinder
Beijing, China

This was a standard extraction mission, in a country that was anything but. The Invincible team, as we'd begun calling ourselves, was brought in by Z Alexander to extract a missing MI6 agent, two CIA operatives, and a high-ranking British diplomat. The four were last seen in Hong Kong, but we'd received intel that they were now being held in China's capital.

As part of a complex negotiation, a meeting was scheduled to take place at the Great Hall of the People, a state building located at the western edge of Tiananmen Square in Beijing.

During that meeting, the UK and US ambassadors to China would publicly announce the exchange of seven Chinese dissidents who had been given asylum in our respective countries, for the four men we were there to extract.

However, that would never happen. Instead, the minute the ambassadors and Chinese officials began their introductions, Edge and Rile would get word to extract the agents from where they were being held, while I intercepted and retrieved the diplomat.

There were four other agents responsible for ensuring the ambassadors' safe transport once the Chinese realized what was happening.

My part of the mission went off without a hitch; I was escorting the man in my charge into the waiting armored transport when I heard Rile shout through the earpiece. *"Got 'em."* It was followed a few seconds later by, *"We're out."*

The transmission should've ended then, but it didn't. The diplomat had just gotten into the transport when I heard several rounds of gunfire.

"Man down!" shouted Rile. I slammed the door closed behind the diplomat and raced in the direction of the predetermined exit point, arriving just as Rile stormed out with Edge in his arms.

I heard the familiar sound of a helicopter landing—it had to be a cobra—and watched as my best friend's body was handed off to a medic. Moments after Rile and I climbed in behind him, the chopper took off.

"Lynx," I said through the mic. "If you can hear this, this is Grinder. Edge was hit, but he's alive. The bullet penetrated his right arm. I'm with him, and we're transporting your brother to Seoul."

"Good, copy," I heard Lynx respond.

"The others?" I asked Rile, who had his hand on his earpiece.

"Mission successful," he reported. "Four subjects along with both ambassadors and additional agents are being transported by Chinook."

"What about Lynx?"

"As soon as they're able, they'll get him to Seoul."

When I first went to work for MI5, after my stint in rehab, Lynx had come to me and asked if I'd be willing to be the second person listed on Edge's medical power of attorney. Given their parents had been killed in a car accident when he and Edge were teenagers, I immediately agreed.

Doing so meant that until Lynx arrived in South Korea, I would be the one giving the doctors the okay to do whatever was necessary to make sure my friend both lived and had use of his arm.

Three weeks later, Edge was stable enough to be transported from Seoul to a hospital in London. There, his doctors anticipated he'd require at least one additional surgery, potentially more, in order to regain full use of his hand.

The man was the orneriest wanker I'd ever known. I wondered if I'd been just as bad. Worse, probably.

"Exponentially worse, actually," Carson said when he met us at the hospital, and I asked.

I'd contacted him to see if he did the type of rehab Edge would require, and was pleased to find out he did. I immediately hired him, knowing if he could put up with me, he could handle my best friend.

"Thanks for meeting me for lunch," my sister said the day after I'd arrived back in London. "How's Edge?"

I told her about his attitude. "He's a bloody wanker."

"No wonder you are such good friends."

I gave her a scowl and picked up the menu.

"Miles, have you talked to Pia recently?"

"I have not."

"Do you intend to?"

I set the menu down. "Why do you ask?"

She shrugged. "I think you should. In fact, I think she may be on her way here as we speak."

"Here?"

"London."

"I see. Did you happen to mention I'd be here?"

"No, Miles. I haven't spoken to her in several days, but when I last did, she gave me the dates she'd be in town."

"What's the reason for her visit?"

"A business trip is my understanding, but, Miles, she isn't traveling alone."

I scrubbed my face with my hand. "Get to the point, Lily."

"She's coming here with someone named Paolo."

Paolo? Could it be the same wanker she was dating when we first met? The one she ran into the night of Lily and Wills' wedding celebration and my homecoming party? The same night Pia had changed my life forever? "He's married. Perhaps, as you said, it's a business trip."

Lily peered up at me. "If he was, he isn't any longer."

"What makes you say that?"

"I got the impression they were dating."

I sat back in my chair and attempted to tamp down the anger and jealousy I felt the moment my sister said Paolo's name.

Did I have any right to feel this way? Wasn't Pia free to live her life as she saw fit? The last time I saw her was the day she dropped me off at rehab for my opioid addiction, and that was over two years ago. We'd written letters—sporadically, on my part in particular—but neither of us mentioned trying to see each other again.

"Contact her, Miles."

"Is that fair, Lil?"

"If I were you, I wouldn't give a rat's if it was fair. If you care about her and want her in your life, fight for her, Miles."

I rested my elbows on the table and looked into my sister's eyes. "What do I have to offer Pia? What kind of life?" I spoke barely above a whisper, but when Lily's eyes filled with tears, I knew she heard me.

"Everything, Miles. All you have to do is want it."

Rather than going straight back to the hospital when our lunch ended, I walked around London, eventually making my way to the hotel where Pia showed me my life wasn't over in the way I'd believed it was.

I walked inside, over to the bar, and ordered a pint. Lily didn't say Pia was staying here, and if she had, I couldn't say for certain I'd be here.

I found an empty table and sat with my head in my hands. Was Lily right? Could Pia and I be together? How? I could never ask her to leave Valentini, and even if I did, what kind of life could I promise her?

Of the four Invincible partners, only Decker was in a relationship, but then his base had always been in Texas, where he and his wife lived. How many other agents did I know who were in relationships? Not many.

The ones I'd worked with at SIS, who I knew were married, had mostly retired, but wasn't I also retired? Wasn't part of being independent being able to accept missions as well as decline them?

My mobile vibrated, and I pulled it out of my pocket.

"I'm at the hospital, waiting for your return," said Rile.

"I'd no idea you were in town."

"Lynx said you left some time ago."

"I stopped for a pint."

"Where?"

I gave Rile the name of the hotel, which wasn't more than a ten-minute walk away. "We could meet elsewhere. There's obviously something urgent—"

"I'm on my way."

The call ended. *What in the bloody hell?*

I'd never quite been able to figure Rile out; the man was an enigma. When he'd brush his bottom lip with the tip of his finger, or smile in that weird way he did, there were times I could swear he was reading my mind. I shuddered at the thought, given there were plenty of instances when the only thing on my mind was what a wanker he could be.

He walked in and sat across the table from me. Within seconds, the barmaid approached to take his order. I shook my head. I hadn't seen her walk from behind the bar a single time since I arrived, and there were plenty of tables waiting.

"I'll have what he's having."

When she walked away, Rile's gaze remained on her arse. When she was out of sight, he turned to me and smiled.

"How are you, Grinder?"

"As well as can be expected."

"Edge will regain full use of his arm."

"Yeah? Can you see into the future, Rile?"

"At times," he answered without missing a beat.

"What about me? What will I be doing say…a year from now?"

He raised a brow, rested his arms on the table, and leaned forward. "I don't think you're ready for me to tell you, but soon, you might be."

"You're a bit up yourself, mate."

He shrugged as though that wasn't news.

"Why are you really here, Rile?"

"What's on your mind?"

"You're answering my question with a question."

He nodded. "It's evident there's something you want to discuss with me."

I shook my head and laughed.

"I'm here, Grinder. Speak."

I stared into my beer and then looked up at him. "Okay. What if one of us wants to be in a relationship? A long-term one?"

"One of us is—Decker is married."

"You know what I mean. Edge, you, me?"

"Why did you join the British Army?"

"To protect and serve," I answered without hesitation.

"Perhaps if you never saw yourself married, you might have considered the priesthood, then?"

"Where are you going with this?"

He sat back in his chair when the barmaid returned with his pint, and then once again watched her as she walked away.

"You, of all people, should be aware of how precious life is. You didn't ask, but the reason I joined SIS was because I believe every man and woman should be able to live their life free of tyranny, free of persecution, free of fear."

I nodded, feeling a little embarrassed that, like he said, I hadn't asked.

"What do you want out of life, Grinder? Work alone? Is that the only way you see yourself? You come from a nice family, no?"

"A very nice family."

"Why wouldn't that be something you'd want?"

I turned my head when someone familiar caught my eye. Walking in the hotel's entrance was the only woman with whom I'd ever imagined building a life. As my sister had warned, she wasn't alone. The man she was with, Paolo, had his arm around her shoulders.

He said something, she laughed, he pulled her close, and kissed her cheek.

Seeing her happy should've made me happy as well. It didn't. Instead, it felt like the bottom had just dropped out of my life, sending me plummeting into a hole I'd never be able to crawl out of.

15

I felt him before I saw him. Mylos was here. I turned my head, just slightly, and saw him seated at a table in the bar with another man whose back was to me. He didn't look up; I didn't know whether he'd seen me walk in.

"Everything okay?" Paolo asked.

"*Sì.* I thought I saw an old friend." I let my gaze rest on the man who'd held my heart since we were both sixteen years old. Seeing him here, now, was like an omen.

As I let Paolo lead me away, I turned my head once more and looked over my shoulder. Mylos' head was raised and our eyes met.

"Paolo, *mi scusi.*" I pointed in the direction of the ladies' room. I walked away slowly, afraid to look behind me a second time.

I let cool water pool in my palms and brought it to my face and then to the back of my neck. I took several deep breaths while I looked at my reflection in the mirror. I'd dreamed of Mylos last night, and it left me feeling unsettled. He was angry with me. He'd shouted his words at me, none of which I could remember when I woke. I'd never known him to raise his voice. He'd never spoken a word to me in real anger. He'd scolded me all those years ago when I tried to use him to make Paolo jealous. How ironic that the three of us were in the same place at the same time once again.

I leaned forward and used the tip of my finger to wipe away the mascara that had run, then washed and dried my hands. When I came out of the ladies' room and looked over to the bar, the table where I'd seen Mylos sat empty.

"Here you are," said Paolo, handing me a small envelope and leading me to the elevator. He pressed the button for the tenth floor, and the door closed, leaving us alone.

"You're on ten, I'm on nine, unless you'd like to switch. The rooms are identical."

"Thank you for honoring my request, Paolo."

"Separate rooms?"

"*Sì.* "

He leaned against the elevator wall and rested the back of his hand on his forehead. "You continue to resist me, but soon, I'll win you over. If it's the last thing I do. Until then, I will remain your devoted servant."

I smiled and swatted his arm. *"Sciocchino."*

"We'll meet in the lobby at seven?" he asked after walking me to my room.

"Thank you again, Paolo, for allowing me to come with you on this trip."

"Sweet, sweet Pia. The pleasure is all mine."

We had a dinner meeting scheduled for eight with the Fellwood Group, the largest wine and spirit distributor in the UK. If they were to add our wine to their list, that alone would give me the sales I needed not only to keep Valentini afloat, but to implement some of the other ideas I'd been toying with.

Throughout the meal, I found my thoughts drifting to Mylos. Why had he been in the bar of our hotel? Had Lily told him I was visiting London? I hadn't told her where I was staying.

"Pia?" Paolo touched my arm.

"Pardon?"

"Mr. Fell asked what your current production levels are for Brunello di Montalcino and Rosso di Montalcino."

"Ten thousand cases each, at the DOCG level, of course."

Mr. Fell and his colleague, Mr. Wood, raised a brow.

"Additionally, fifteen thousand cases each of Brunellos and Brunello Riservas."

"Impressive. Paolo, these numbers are higher than yours," said Mr. Wood.

"If I may, while production may seem high for these particular wines, unlike Viticcio, we only grow Sangiovese."

The rest of the dinner conversation was focused on more of the same, and at the end, the gentlemen from Fellwood promised we'd hear from them in the next few days with an order.

"This is fantastic," said Paolo on the cab ride back to the hotel.

"It is." I tried to match his enthusiasm, but until I saw what the orders were, I was hesitant to celebrate.

"What do you say we have a nightcap?" he asked as we walked into the hotel.

"Thank you, Paolo, but I am very tired. I think I'll call it a night. Thank you again for all you've done for Valentini."

"I'll ride up with you." He put his arm around my shoulders and squeezed. "We make a good team, Pia." As we waited for the elevator, he lowered his lips to mine. I tried to back away, but with his arm around my neck, I couldn't, so I turned my face. "Paolo, please."

"I thought perhaps, since dinner went so well, you would be in the mood to…thank me."

"In the mood to thank you? What does that mean?"

"It seems only fair." He leaned closer, and I could smell the alcohol on his breath. He grasped my arm hard enough that I knew tomorrow I'd have bruises. "You owe me, Pia."

"I owe you? What am I, a whore whose wine you've pimped to your customers?"

He tightened his grasp. "You're making far too much of this, *amore mio*."

Even if we hadn't been the only people in the elevator, I still would've done the same thing. I raised my hand and slapped him.

"Was that necessary?" He rubbed his cheek.

I wrenched my arm from his grip. "I'm going to give you the benefit of the doubt, Paolo, since you've never behaved this way with me before, and assume you are drunk." The elevator door opened, and I stepped out, barring his exit. "Good night, Paolo. If you want to remain my friend, tomorrow I'll expect an apology, after which we'll never speak of this again." When the doors started to close, I took a step back, not hearing whatever he said in response.

I stalked to my room, fuming at what a disaster the night had been. I was disappointed beyond belief that what should have been the end of a nice evening, had turned so unpleasant.

I'd just stepped from the shower when I heard a knock at the door. "This is ridiculous," I muttered, donning the white terry-cloth robe the hotel provided.

I pulled the door open in anger, prepared to tear into the man who was quickly becoming my former friend. "I'm in no mood for this, Paolo—"

"Lover's spat?" Mylos smirked and rested one arm on the doorjamb. "You should know, he left the hotel only moments ago with a very tall, very beautiful blonde."

"Thank you for delivering that information to me personally; however, what Mr. Viticcio does in his free time is of no interest to me."

Mylos pushed past me.

"*Mi scusi*, I did not invite you in."

"I thought maybe since you and *Mr. Viticcio* have such an *open* relationship, I'd keep you company in his absence."

"This is getting old," I muttered under my breath as I stalked over to him and raised my hand to slap his face like I had Paolo's. Mylos, though, was too quick for me. He leaned forward, close enough to kiss me, and stared into my eyes.

I wrenched my arm away and rubbed my wrist. "Why are you here, Mylos?"

"I can't believe you're with him. What happened to his wife? Are you the reason they divorced? Are you a homewrecker, Pia?"

"It's time for you to leave." I walked over to the door and held it open for him.

"I just have one question—"

I slammed the door closed. "What?"

"I mean that little to you, Pia?"

I shook my head. "*You mean that little to me? I am nothing to you. Nothing!* I am the pretty Italian girl you bump into every couple of years, have a quick fuck, and then I never hear from you again."

"That's rich, coming from you."

I scrunched my eyes. "What does that mean?"

"Whenever we're together, you can't get back to Italy fast enough."

"It's where I live, Mylos." I walked over and poured a shot of whatever brown liquor was in the decanter. Holding my breath, I downed it. My throat burned and I coughed.

"Jesus," he said, stalking over to me. He pulled the glass from my hand, reached into the bar refrigerator, and put a few ice cubes in it before pouring more of the liquor.

"No, thank you," I said when he tried to hand it to me. He drank it himself. "Don't you think you've already had enough?"

"Are you suggesting I'm drunk?"

"What else would explain you barging in here like a madman?"

"The last drink I had was hours ago when you came waltzing in with your boyfriend and then proceeded to waltz out on your date. Don't think I missed the kiss in the elevator either."

"Have you been *watching* me?"

"Sì," he said, mimicking me and making me itch to slap him again. Not that I did the first time, but I'd meant to. Instead, I put my hand on my heart.

Like in my dream, Mylos and I were shouting at each other. A profound sadness swept over me. I sat down on the sofa and put my head in my hands. "Please leave, Mylos. Just go away. We never have to see each other again."

"Is it really that easy for you?"

I stared up at him. "What are you talking about?"

"To say you never want to see me again?"

"That isn't what I said." I put my face back in my hands, hiding my tears as I wept.

"Fuck!" he growled as he sat down beside me, pulling my hand from my face, gently this time.

I couldn't look at him. My heart was breaking, and to look at his beautiful face, maybe for the last time, was more than I could stand.

The last thing I expected was for him to pull me into his arms, but that's what he did. He held me close to him, murmuring to me as I cried.

"I can't do this, Mylos."

He put his hand on my chin and raised my face. "Do what, Pia?"

"I can't fight with you. I can't stand hearing you raise your voice at me. It hurts too much. The things you said to me…is that how you see me?" I stood up, weaving my fingers into my hair. "Who am I that two men in one night see me so differently than I see myself?"

He stood too and put his hands on my arms, gently lowering them. "I'm sorry. I was, I am…jealous."

"But why? Why are you jealous of someone you don't even care about?"

"What makes you think I don't care?"

"If I hadn't come to London with Paolo, when would I have seen you again?"

He let go and turned his back on me. "Would you believe that's all I've been thinking about, even before I saw you walk in earlier?"

"No."

"I didn't think so, but it's true. When Lily told me you were traveling with a man…I couldn't stand it."

"Because you were jealous?"

"Yes."

"At least you're being honest. But, Mylos, you can't just want me when you think someone else does."

He turned back toward me and pulled me into his arms. "I know. I've handled things with you so badly. Like I said, Lily told me earlier that you were coming to town with Paolo. After she did, I took a long walk, and it led me here. I had no idea if you were staying in this hotel, and I wasn't even sure that's why I came. It was more that this place will always remind me it was you, Pia, who made me whole again."

"I don't want your gratitude, Mylos."

"Can we sit?"

I nodded and sat down first.

Mylos took my hand in his. "It isn't gratitude. That's far too small a word for how I feel. What you did for me, it was everything, Pia. *Everything.* Do you understand?"

"And still, it wasn't enough."

"Why do you say that?"

I shook my head. I couldn't spell it out for him. That was the whole point. He didn't get it, because I didn't matter to him in the same way he mattered to me. I loved him. I'd known it for years, pushed it away, but it always came back.

Even if this would be the last time, I wanted us to make love. Tomorrow, I would get on a plane and return to Val d'Orcia to stay. The Valentini name would end with me, and maybe then, so would the curse.

Our lovemaking was soft and sweet, as though we both knew it was goodbye. We didn't speak, and when it was over, I rolled on my side and pretended to sleep. I was still awake over an hour later when he crept from the bed and quietly left.

16

Grinder

"Forgive me, my friend. If it was not a true emergency, I would not have bothered you," Rile said when I met him downstairs in the lobby after receiving the SOS alert.

Thankfully, Pia was asleep when I left. I wedged a stop in the lock and hoped to be back in her bed before she woke and realized I was gone.

"What is it?"

"A possible kidnapping."

I scrubbed my face with my hand. "Who?"

"Someone with close ties to the Monarchy."

Instead of returning to Pia's bed, I spent the next several days traveling with Rile from London to Budapest and finally to America. We'd been forced to go deep undercover; if word had gotten out that the woman was kidnapped, the media attention alone would've ensured we never would've found her—alive anyway.

Now that she was safely ensconced back with her family, Rile and I were in Texas, awaiting Edge's arrival.

I'd been trying to reach Pia for several days to explain, but was unsuccessful. I could only imagine what she was thinking, particularly given the conversation we'd had earlier that evening. My intention was to leave in the next couple of days and travel directly to Italy. If all else failed, I'd show up on her doorstep and beg her forgiveness.

Instead, when Edge and his brother arrived at the King-Alexander Ranch late this evening, I found myself thrust into yet another mission. This time, on behalf of my best friend.

A member of the Aryan Brotherhood of Texas was murdered shortly after we left for Beijing. The woman charged with the crime was someone Edge had met the night before we left, and having come face-to-face with the dead bloke, he felt responsible.

The ABT was a nasty bunch of fuckers with a slew of enemies. The hard part, though, was figuring out which of those enemies had executed the hit, and then proving it. With any gang-related crime, that was the ultimate challenge.

I knew immediately that this investigation was personal for Edge. "What do you see happening with this woman?" I asked a few days into it. It took him a long time to answer.

"I don't know."

"Not good, mate."

"Rebel doesn't have anyone else who can help her."

I nodded. "So you're the white knight."

"I can't explain it, Grind. When I met her, something just clicked. It's more than that she's hot as fuck."

"You're arse over elbows."

He smiled. "That, I am."

He wasn't the only one. The raw vulnerability Pia had revealed to me when we were last together, struck me square in the heart. I too wanted to be her white knight, even though I was the one from whom she needed saving. The things I said to her still rolled around in my gut, shaming me.

And then, while she slept, I left. It didn't occur to me I wouldn't be back. If it had, I would've woken her. Instead, I'd had to go completely dark. I shook my head. What she must think. I needed to call Lily.

Asking my sister to intervene on my behalf was going to cost me, both in pride and also in the jabs my sister would inflict on me. It would be worth it, though, considering I had no idea how long our current investigation might take.

17

Pia

It had been three weeks since I took an early flight back from London. For the first seven days straight, I received a flower delivery from Paolo. They only stopped when I finally agreed to see him, mainly because it meant he'd forgone the second leg of his sales trip to return to Italy.

Since I'd offered to never mention his behavior again if he apologized, for my own conscience, I had to honor it.

"Will you give me another chance?" he'd begged.

I told him I forgave him, but our friendship—not that friendship was the chance he was asking for—would never be the same.

He'd offered again to represent Valentini in his future sales meetings, but I declined. The order we'd received from Fellwood was more than I initially thought it might be, and I hoped their distribution of our wine would continue. Otherwise, feeling beholden to Paolo was a position I'd never put myself in again.

When he left, he vowed he wouldn't give up. Someday, some way, he'd make it up to me, he'd promised. I didn't bother to tell him there was nothing he could do. He already knew that.

I had no expectation that I'd hear from Mylos, and yet I was still disappointed. It was better this way. It would take time, but I'd get over him. It wasn't as though he was a daily part of my life anyway. The idea that I'd never see him again was the part that was hardest to accept.

I saw my mother sitting on the *terrazza* and went outside to join her.

"*Buongiorno,* Mamma." I kissed her cheek.

"*Buongiorno,* Pia."

"How are you feeling this morning?"

"A bit better."

It had been weeks, maybe months, that my mother was ill. I'd taken her to see the doctor several times, but they found no reason for her to be as sick as she was.

"No more flowers?" she asked.

I laughed. "I think Paolo has finally given up."

From where we sat, we could see Georgio arriving at the winery. He was on the phone, and he didn't look happy.

"Have you spoken with Nonna Bella?" I asked.

My mamma shook her head.

"Are you concerned?"

She looked over her shoulder toward the house. "I don't understand why she'd stop communicating after all the years she's been with us. I've asked Georgio, and he said she's recovering."

I'd done the same. I'd also asked Gabriella, whose mother was supposedly caring for Nonna Bella. She said the same thing Georgio had.

Even Lucia's mother, who'd worked side by side our long-time cook, had nothing to report on her friend's well-being.

"Good morning," said Lucia, joining us a few minutes later on the *terrazza*.

"*Buongiorno.* I was just thinking about your mamma. How is she?"

"A bit better." Lucia had taken over her mother's duties the last couple of weeks, saying that, like my mother, Nonna Carina was feeling under the weather.

She asked if she could bring us anything, and we both thanked her and declined.

"Mamma?" I began after Lucia went back inside. "What would happen with the estate if I never had a child?"

"I've never thought about it." She reached over and took my hand. "I'm sorry things didn't work out with you and Paolo."

I didn't tell her I wasn't thinking about him. The less I said about Mylos, the better.

"I'm sure you will meet someone else, Pia. He will be the person you're meant to be with. These things cannot be rushed. Look at your papà and me. I was not much younger than you are when we met."

"I know you're right, Mamma, but the curse still worries me. If I don't have an heir and someone else inherits Valentini, do you think Estancia's curse will finally end?"

"What I think is you are being silly and overly dramatic. However, if you do not have an heir, there will be no one else to inherit. I do not have any siblings, and neither did my mother, nor her mother before her. Or before that."

"Are you saying that there were no male heirs?"

"None after Estancia."

"And no one had more than one child?"

"As far as I know. Even Estancia had only one daughter."

"This is unbelievable. I need to know, Mamma, what happens if I never have a child?"

"I've already told you, Pia, I don't know. I suppose the estate would have to be sold." She rubbed her temples. "I don't understand why you're so worried about this. You will meet someone new. You'll get married, have a baby or maybe many babies, and this conversation will be for nothing."

When I left my mother and went back to the winery office, Georgio was waiting for me. I didn't like the look on his face and wasn't in the mood for another argument, especially after the frustrating conversation I'd just had with my mother.

"What can I do for you?" I asked.

"We may have trouble fulfilling the order you wrote without consulting me."

My head snapped up. "What do you mean? Our production levels are far above what was ordered."

"There's an issue with the vintages."

"An issue? You are bitching that I didn't consult you about an order, but you haven't informed me of an issue with our inventory?"

"Never mind."

"*What?* What do you mean never mind? Explain, Georgio."

He stomped out of the office, leaving me with my mouth hanging open. I was so furious I was having trouble breathing. I should fire him on the spot, but until I had someone else lined up to replace him, I couldn't afford to do that.

Georgio came back a few days later, saying he was mistaken and we would have no trouble with the order. We'd been friends all of our lives, and yet, he felt like a stranger to me—one I couldn't trust.

I'd placed a call to Mateo when Georgio first told me about the still-unnamed "issue," but didn't reach him. When he called back several days later, he was apologetic.

"Do you think I'm being paranoid, Mateo?" I asked after telling him how the conversation with Georgio went.

He didn't answer right away, and I wondered if our call had disconnected. "It would be best if you didn't let him go right now."

"Why?"

He breathed out a heavy sigh. "Try to make things work for now."

"Do you think he'll intentionally do something to jeopardize our business?"

"I do not."

He sounded emphatic, and I trusted my cousin. His explanation that he'd been away and unable to be reached seemed very unusual, though. Once again, I felt as though things in my world were off-kilter.

On top of everything else, I wasn't feeling well. Sometimes I felt perfectly fine. Others, I couldn't keep any food down. All I could think was that I was coming down with whatever ailed my mother and Nonna Carina.

I went upstairs to lie down, and the minute my head hit the pillow, I felt nauseous. I barely made it to the lavatory before I lost the contents of my stomach.

I stayed in bed most of the rest of the day, even when I began feeling better, wondering if Estancia was trying to give me warnings not to doubt her curse. What else could explain how many things seemed to be going wrong in my life?

When my cell phone rang, later in the day, I hesitated when I saw Lily's name pop up, but it wasn't her fault Mylos was no longer in my life.

"How are you, Lily?"

"Exhausted, Pia. How are you?"

"A bit under the weather, but otherwise okay."

She asked what was wrong, and I explained my symptoms.

She laughed. "The last time I felt that way, I was pregnant."

"That isn't my problem. Unless it is an immaculate conception. How are the kids?"

"Angus is almost as tall as I am. Aria is my little angel, and baby Miles is colicky."

I'd forgotten she and Wills mentioned naming their third child after her brother, even though Angus' middle name was the same. "What does that mean?" I asked, hoping her answer would get my mind off the pain in my heart whenever I thought about Mylos.

My heart sunk when I received an email from Fellwood not long after, canceling their order, citing a concern over our "quality issues."

To make matters worse, earlier in the week, Georgio came to me to say the corking machine had broken down. Replacing it would cost more than 10,000 euros.

Not to mention, I still wasn't feeling better. Overcome, I put my head in my hands and cried. My cell phone rang; Lily was calling again.

"Hi."

"You don't sound good."

Ten minutes later, I finished unloading the shitstorm my life had become.

"I'm sorry, Pia. I wish you felt you could've confided in me sooner."

"It isn't easy for me." I blew my nose and wiped at my tears.

"I think trying to build a tourism business by advertising the farmhouse is a good idea. As would be adding to the accommodations you offer. It seems like people who visit would also buy wine."

"You would think so, but I have another confession, Lily. The last group who rented the farmhouse for more than one night was your family."

"Can I ask you something?"

Here it came; I knew exactly what she'd ask. "Sure."

"Have you talked to Miles?"

Any hope I had of ebbing the flow of my tears, was lost. Now that I'd started, I might as well continue and tell Lily everything.

"Your brother showed up when I was last in London, and we had a terrible argument."

"About?"

"Paolo, which was none of his business." I told her how after we'd made up and then made love, her brother sneaked out of my room.

"Pia, tell me your symptoms again."

I went through how I felt nauseous several times a day and then, at others, I felt fine. I was tired, but that could easily be explained by the stress I was under.

"Anything else you can think of?"

"No."

"What about your breasts, are they tender?"

Lily's question stunned me, but they were. "Yes."

"Pia, I know you said it was impossible for you to be pregnant, but you just told me you and my brother were together."

"I'm on birth control, Lily."

"It has been known to fail."

I counted back in my head to my last menstrual cycle and gasped.

"I'm sorry, Pia. I know this doesn't help, but if you are pregnant, you should be under a doctor's care."

I nodded but couldn't speak.

"Are you still there?"

"*Sì*. Lily. Promise me you won't tell Mylos."

"I understand why you would say that, but Pia, if you are pregnant and the baby is his, he needs to know."

"I will tell him, but in my own time."

"I get it and promise I won't interfere."

I hung up and dissolved into sobs. How could I be pregnant? I looked up at the ceiling and shook my fist. "If this is your doing, Estancia, I will give you a piece of my mind in the afterlife."

18

Grinder

"Do you have a moment?" my sister asked when I answered her call.

"Of course. Is everything okay?"

"We're all fine, as are Mum and Dad."

Odd way for her to put it. "Is there someone who isn't?"

She sighed. "I'm breaking a confidence, Miles."

"Go on."

"It's Pia."

I scrubbed my face with my hand. "I've been trying to reach her for weeks. Unsuccessfully. I know she's upset about what happened in London, but if she'd only speak to me, I could explain."

"I'm afraid she's going to lose Valentini."

"What do you mean?" As soon as I asked, I recalled Pia telling me she was considering selling.

"Business is bad. Things keep going wrong. I think she's been struggling since her father died."

"She mentioned selling. Is that still a viable option?"

"Miles!"

"What?"

"How can you suggest she let Valentini go?"

"I'm sorry, Lil, but I don't know what you expect me to do."

"I was thinking that if you were coming home for Christmas, our family could come up with ways to try to help her."

"I wasn't planning on it."

"I don't know why I bothered to call you. Pia told me you didn't give a rat's about her, and I guess she was right. Happy Christmas, Miles."

The call ended, and I knew it wasn't because it had dropped.

Before I got involved in Edge's mission, my intention had been to go to Italy to explain what happened in London. Was there anything stopping me from going now? I rang Lily back, hoping she'd answer. "I'll see what I can do."

"You'll come home for Christmas?"

"I was thinking of going straight to Valentini."

"That would be brilliant, Miles. I've another idea. This is about the farmhouse."

"Go on."

I'd just set a packed bag by the front door when I heard a knock.

"I've come to talk to you about Christmas," said Edge when he came inside. "Going somewhere?" He pointed at my bag.

"Have a seat."

"I don't want to keep you."

"I'm leaving for a while, Edge. I don't know exactly how long I'll be gone."

"Are you okay?"

I nodded. "It's Pia."

"Is she okay?"

"My sister fears she's about to lose the winery that's been in her family dating back to the mid-fifteen hundreds. My gut, though, is telling me there's something more to it."

"Like?"

"Her father's accident, primarily."

"Are you bloody serious?" he exclaimed when I told him Pia's father had been run over by a forklift.

It was cold as hell the night I left the ranch to catch a flight to Italy. This kind of weather exacerbated the pain and discomfort of my skin graft. Whoever said that what I experienced was psychosomatic, as some doctors did, should keep their opinions to themselves unless they'd suffered through the same trauma as people like me had.

I turned on the news station as I drove to the Austin-Bergstrom International Airport. Evidently, it hadn't snowed in this area in ten years. Ten years. I met Pia ten years ago. God, what a lot had happened in that time. Our lives had completely changed. Mine far more than hers, although was that fair? She'd lost her father, and if what my sister told me was true, she may be about to lose her home.

Travel time to Florence was over fifteen hours, including a layover in Frankfurt. By the time I reached Valentini, it would be Christmas. I wished I'd thought to bring Pia a gift. A real gift. Not something I picked up at the Frankfurt airport.

I settled into my sleeper seat, hoping I would be able to stop my brain from coming up with scenarios or theories as to what Pia was up against.

"Can I get you anything, Mr. Stone?" asked the flight attendant. A sleeping pill would be nice. Not that she could or that I would ask.

I'd hired a car and was on my way from Florence to Val d'Orcia when my sister rang to wish me a happy Christmas. Hearing all the noise in the background, I regretted not being with them, especially with my nephews and niece.

"Are you on your way to Valentini?" she asked.

"About an hour away."

"I'm glad you made the trip, Miles. Oh, and as a reminder, the farmhouse is under Wills' parents' name."

"George and Mary Spencer?" It had been my sister's idea to put the rental in their name so I could surprise Pia with my arrival.

I pulled up to the gate and gave George's name to the person who spoke through the intercom. She told me to come to the main house to collect the key since the winery, where I'd normally pick it up, was closed.

Now, I just had to hope that Pia answered the door.

I parked the car near the entrance to the winery and pulled out the box I carried in my pocket. I opened the hinge and fingered the five-carat pear-shaped ruby that hung from a chain of oval and rondelle ruby beads.

I'd rung Rile to tell him I was on my way to Italy and would be taking a leave from the Invincibles. He wouldn't accept my leave but did promise he would not call on me for any further missions until I was ready.

I wished him a happy Christmas, and he'd asked what gift I was giving Pia. When I shared my plight, he gave me the name of an old friend, who he was certain would have something perfect for her. After insisting I write down the address, he said the gentleman would be expecting me.

With a three-hour layover in Frankfurt, I hired a driver. There were times Rile was truly eerie, a belief reinforced when the jeweler showed me the necklace that was now in my possession.

"How did you know?" I'd asked.

He smiled, but didn't answer. It couldn't have been that Rile gave him any tips. He didn't know about the stone I carried in my pocket, nor had he ever met Pia.

I recognized the woman who answered the door. "Lucia, right?"

She looked at the paper in her hand and then back at me. "George Spencer?"

I laughed. "Actually, I'm Miles Stone. I stayed here several years ago and wanted to surprise Pia; the reservation is in a family member's name. She doesn't happen to be about, does she?"

"I believe *Signora* Deltetto has retired for the evening, but in the morning, I'll let her know you asked for her."

I'd hoped to see her tonight, but given the lateness of the hour, I understood.

"One more thing," I said before she closed the door. "You wouldn't happen to have a bottle of wine I could purchase?"

"I'm sorry, but I don't. Tomorrow—"

I held up my hand. "Right. My apologies. I keep forgetting it's Christmas."

19

Pia

Stepping from a corner of the *terrazza*, I gripped the back of the chair and then sat down. Mylos was here. Why?

The only reason I could think of was that Lily had done the one thing I'd begged her not to. She told him I was pregnant.

I didn't go inside. Instead, I went down to the winery and grabbed a bottle of wine. Since it was unseasonably warm for the end of December—which was why I'd been sitting outside—I walked to the farmhouse.

In the still darkness of night, I rubbed my belly, talking to the *bambino* growing inside me.

I wished Lily hadn't told her brother about the baby. It wasn't her place. I told her I'd do it in my own time, and I meant it. For this, I'd never forgive her.

I took a deep breath and knocked on the door.

"Hello, Mylos," I said when it opened.

"Pia." He opened the door wider. "Please come in."

I stepped around him and then handed him the bottle of wine.

"Thank you. Lucia told you." He led me into the kitchen. "Would you like a glass?"

Was he testing me? "No, thank you."

"How are you?" he asked, leading me back out of the kitchen and into the sitting room.

"Why are you here?"

"To see you, Pia. I—"

"Why else?" I pressed, wanting to get this conversation over with as quickly as possible. The baby—the one he and I had made together—wasn't his responsibility. I would raise the heir to Valentini on my own. The sooner he knew that, the better.

I sat down, and he sat next to me. "There's something I need to say to you."

I leaned back and folded my arms.

"I'm sorry. I know that doesn't begin to ease the pain I caused you when I left the night we were last together. If I'd had any idea what I was walking into, I would've woken you to say goodbye. My intention was to come back without you ever knowing I was gone." He reached forward and put his hand on my arm. "That ended up being impossible for me to do, and I'm sorry."

I moved my arm away from his reach. He could've contacted me the next morning, left a message, sent me a note, but he'd done none of those things.

"I was glad you left."

His eyes opened wide.

"That night, our lovemaking, it was me saying goodbye to you, Mylos. I thought you understood and that was why you left."

"I don't believe you." He tried to reach for me again, but I swatted his hand away.

"I don't care."

"I'm here to help you, Pia."

Il bastardo arrogante.

"I don't need your help, now or ever, which means you can leave. I'll refund the money you paid. The sooner you realize I intend to do this on my own, the easier it will be for you to walk away."

He cocked his head. "I know you're struggling, Pia. Are you really willing to lose Valentini because you're too proud to accept my help?"

"That isn't what I'm talking about, and you know it."

He leaned forward and put his elbows on his knees.

"I should go." I stood to leave, but he grabbed my wrist.

"Please don't. There's something I want to give you." He pulled a small box from his pocket.

"No!" I exclaimed. "Please don't do this." My shock quickly turned to embarrassment when he opened the lid and held it out to me.

"Happy Christmas."

I touched the single pear-shaped stone with my fingertip.

"The minute I saw it, I knew it should belong to you."

I looked into his eyes. "I can't accept it."

He set the box on the table. "I know I hurt you, but if you'd let me explain exactly what happened, maybe somewhere in your heart, you can find forgiveness."

"Why won't you just be honest? Why won't you admit the real reason you're here?"

He stood in front of me. "As I said, there are many reasons. Your forgiveness is the most important to me."

"Why? If you think I'm going to let you take…" I dissolved into tears and turned my back to him.

"I would never take Valentini from you, Pia. I want to help you keep it."

Why was he being so relentless? In the back of my mind, I wondered if I was wrong and he didn't know about the baby. But it was the only explanation for him being here that made sense.

"Pia, I talked to Lily."

I took a deep breath and held it.

"I know you're struggling to keep the estate going. You admitted that to me yourself. Let me help."

"What makes you think you can just wave your hand and fix it?"

"I don't think that at all. I'm here for you. That's it. Just you."

"*Just* me?" I smirked.

"Yes, Pia. Just you."

I closed my eyes and took a deep breath. "Not the baby?"

I knew immediately that Lily hadn't betrayed my confidence. Mylos gripped the back of the sofa, and his eyes darted back and forth. Finally, he looked into mine. "Baby?"

"Your baby."

He sat down and dropped his arms to his sides. I could see he was processing what I'd told him. Soon, his questions would start.

"I never dreamed…"

"I want you to know I was on birth control. I don't know why it didn't work. I would never try to trap or trick you."

"I know you wouldn't."

He looked from my eyes down my body. "How do you feel?"

"Better now, but it comes and goes."

"Are you seeing a doctor?"

I nodded.

"You thought that was the reason I was here?"

"*Sì.*"

"No wonder you didn't want to talk to me. I had no idea. I swear. If I had…I would've come sooner. I know that sounds bloody awful, but I would've come for you, Pia. Not just for the baby."

I sat down and turned my body so I was facing him. "Tell me what happened that night."

He scrubbed his face with his hand and then rested his head on the sofa and looked up at the ceiling. "I got an SOS alert. It isn't something we take lightly, nor do we use it unnecessarily. If anyone on our team receives an SOS, it means to act immediately."

I nodded.

"The alert was followed by a message from Rile saying he was in the hotel lobby. My intention was to find out what it was and then come back. In hindsight, that was foolish of me. It should have been a logical assumption that if I received a distress call, a mission was imminent. That was the case. We left immediately."

"Why didn't you contact me?"

"There are some ops where we simply can't. Usually, as was the case with this one, any contact might jeopardize the person we're trying to rescue or protect. We went completely dark, meaning undercover. After it was over and I *could* contact you, I tried. Countless times."

I couldn't look at him and confess what I'd done, so I turned my head. "I blocked your number."

"I figured that out eventually. In fact, I'd planned to come to Italy at the end of November, but the night before I intended to leave, our team was pulled into another investigation." He picked up the box that held the necklace. "Can I put this on you?"

"I don't have a gift for you."

"You gave me the best gift of my life, Pia. In fact, you've done so many times. I don't know that I'd be here, on this earth, if it weren't for your gifts."

"I haven't done anything, Mylos."

He fastened the ruby strand around my neck. My hair was already brushed to the side, so he kissed below my ear. A shudder ran the length of my body.

20

Grinder

"Can you ever forgive me, Pia?"

"And if I do, what changes, Mylos?"

"What do you mean?"

"You'll be here a few days, and then you'll leave, and maybe we'll see each other again in a couple of years."

"Didn't you see the reservation for the farmhouse? I'll be here at least six months."

"You only did that to be kind because you know I need the money."

I shook my head. "I'm not leaving, Pia. I have a reservation and I'm staying." She didn't believe me, but that was okay. I'd prove more to her with my actions than my words ever could.

I sat down and looked at where her hand rested on her belly. "He or she is ours. Made from you and me." I heard the awe in my own voice, and I took a deep breath. I'd never expected I'd be a father. Sure, somewhere in the back of my mind, I might've hoped for it at one time in my life. That it would be a reality would take some getting used to. "Pia, please let me stay."

I had to figure out a way to convince her that when I got on the plane to come to Italy, I made a decision about her and me. I wanted to be part of her life, a permanent part. I had no idea how we'd accomplish it, but Rile seemed to think it was as easy as making the decision. Why couldn't I be an Invincibles partner and be based out of Italy?

Setting that aside, I needed Pia to tell me about the struggles she was having with Valentini. It might prove to be more difficult than getting information out of an international intelligence agency. If I knew anything about her, and I did, she would hold what she saw as her failures close to her. It would be up to me to convince her she could trust me enough to set aside her pride and confide in me.

"You are deep in thought."

I looked into her eyes. "Remember when I came to Italy to see you and you traveled to London?"

"*Sì.*"

"I hated that we'd…I'd…wasted so much time that I could have spent with you. I feel that way now. Regretful."

"Fantasy and reality can be very different things, Mylos. You have an idea of me, and I of you, that may not be who we really are. You may find that once you spend time with me, the flesh-and-blood Pia isn't the same as the dream Pia."

As she spoke, I thought about arguing with her, saying that I did know her and she knew me. But she was right. The only way for us to know for sure was to spend more than a handful of days together.

"I want to be the man you need. In all ways."

"I worry that if I'm not the woman you need, you won't be honest with me, because of the baby."

"I could have the same worry."

"But you don't?"

I shook my head. "I know you'll tell me the truth. You're incapable of lying."

"Am I?"

"I know you better than you think, Pia."

"I have to go back to the house. My mamma will worry."

"I'll take you."

"I'd rather walk."

"I'll walk with you."

"You aren't going to ask me to stay?"

"I would if I thought that's what you wanted. Instead, I think you want me to prove to you I'm not going anywhere."

"You're going to stay here, in the farmhouse?"

"You say it like it's a bad thing. I love this place." I waved my arm in a sweeping motion. I wasn't lying; I really did love it. A new bed and pillows would be in order if I was going to stay for a few months, but otherwise, this place felt like home.

I walked Pia to the front door of the villa. She bit her lower lip as though she was struggling with something.

"I'll see you tomorrow?"

"Mylos?" She rested the palms of her hands on my arms. "Is this real?"

I leaned down and touched her lips with mine. "Nothing has ever felt more real to me."

I stood outside the door longer than I should have after she closed it. Perhaps somewhere inside of me, I hoped she'd come back out. Finally, I turned and left.

On the walk back, I thought a lot about what *real* meant to me. I'd seen and done more in my lifetime than any man should. Those things, like the explosion, had changed me. I'd suffered through unimaginable pain, got addicted to painkillers, and experienced terrifying nightmares almost every night. *Almost every night.* On the very rare occasions when Pia slept in my arms, I didn't recall dreaming.

When I was with her, I remembered that sixteen-year-old boy who was infatuated to the point of exclusion of everything else. I talked more, laughed more, relaxed more. She brought light into my life, and I vowed I wouldn't bring any more darkness into hers.

Instead of going inside, I stood on the farmhouse *terrazza* and looked up at the night sky. The more time I spent with Pia, the more at peace I felt. The longer I was at Valentini, the more at home I felt.

Climbing the stairs, I knew that regardless of whether another was bigger or more comfortable, I'd sleep in the same room I had ten years ago. The room where I'd looked out the window one day and lost my heart to a beautiful girl whose smile and laughter spoke directly to my soul.

I slept quite late the next morning, by my standards anyway. When I made my way downstairs, I was delighted to find fresh fruit and pastries I didn't recall being there the night before on the counter. I looked over and noticed the door to the *terrazza* was slightly ajar. When I peeked out and saw Pia sitting at the table, I went out to join her.

It was a little nippy, considering I was wearing only flannel trousers—no shirt, no shoes—but just the sight of her warmed me.

"Good morning." I leaned down and kissed her cheek. She looked up at me and smiled.

"Buongiorno."

I noticed she had a plate of fruit on the table in front of her. "What a lovely surprise to have you join me for breakfast."

"I wanted to make sure I wasn't dreaming last night." She reached up and touched the ruby necklace with her fingertips. "I love this," she murmured. "Thank you."

"It looks so beautiful against your skin."

Her cheeks turned pink, and she smiled. "I'm happy you're here, Mylos. I know it didn't sound that way. But I am."

"I sat out here for a few minutes last night, struck by how calm I feel when I'm here. At peace, I suppose."

"You were on holiday the first time. Maybe that's why."

I shook my head. "That's nothing to do with it."

Her eyelids drooped. "What is it, then?"

I took her hand and brought it to my lips. "It's you, Pia. Always you."

"I am not always calm. Or peaceful."

"Is that a warning?"

She nodded and put her hands on her stomach. "I've been reading about having a baby. How it's important to avoid stress." She shook her head. *"Impossibile."*

"That's one of the reasons I'm here. I want to help."

"How? Do you know how to run a winery? Make wine perhaps?"

I held up both my hands. "Absolutely not. The answer to both is no."

She tapped her cheek with her index finger, similar to what my sister, Lily, often did. "You will work in the vineyards, then?"

"I don't think your other workers would welcome me."

"You would be a nice addition to the tasting room."

"Would I?"

"Sì. The lady tourists would love you."

"Even if I know little about wine?"

She laughed. "Especially if you don't."

"Do you know what I'd like to do more than anything else?"

She shook her head. I stood and rested my hands on her shoulders, gently working my fingers into her tight muscles.

"Mmm, that feels so good."

"What I'd like to do more than anything else, is keep the stress away."

"It comes from so many different directions."

"I'll shield you, no matter the direction." I leaned down and kissed the side of her neck, making her moan.

"Mylos?" She turned her head. Our lips were close enough that I could kiss her, but first, I wanted to hear what she had to say. "I'm afraid to believe," she whispered.

"As the sun sets and then rises again, day after day, you'll have more reasons to believe."

"You'll be here?"

"I will. I promise." I didn't make them lightly. Ever. I was too aware of my shortcomings, too aware of the commitments in my life. But being here for her, with her, was a promise I'd never break. Even if it meant leaving the rest of my life behind.

She put her hand on my bare chest. "You're cold."

"I wouldn't be if you let me hold you."

She stood, and I sat in her chair, pulling her onto my lap. I rested my hand on her stomach and looked into her eyes. I wanted so much to tell her I loved her because I did with all my heart. She wouldn't trust it, though. Not yet. First I had to show her, let her feel my love. Then, when I said the words, she'd believe me.

21

Pia

Why couldn't I tell him how I really felt? What was stopping me from simply saying how truly happy I was that he was here with me? That being held in his arms did help take the stress away? Not just with the baby, but with everything.

I loved the feeling of his hand on my stomach. It was as though he wasn't just promising me he'd be here, he was promising the same thing to our baby. What made me think even for a moment that I could do this on my own? More, how could I have been so selfish? Mylos deserved to be part of our baby's life, in the same way he or she would deserve to have a father who was present.

After what happened when I was last in London, a part of me worried I'd wake up one morning and he'd be gone. I feared not being able to reach him, worrying about him, wondering if he was coming back. Only time would tell if my fears would materialize. In the meantime, I couldn't spend every moment doubting him.

"How are you feeling?" he asked.

"Today is better than the last few days."

"You said you've been reading books about having a baby?"

"*Sì*. It feels overwhelming, but then I realize women have been doing this for thousands of years without the benefit of a book to tell them what to expect."

"How many people know you're pregnant?"

"Three. Me, you, and Lily."

He raised his eyebrows. "Lily, but not your mother?"

"Not yet." I couldn't say why I hadn't confided in her. Maybe I was waiting for it to feel more real to me.

"I meant what I said about helping you with Valentini, Pia. All you have to do is tell me what you need."

I smiled. "A couple million euros would come in handy."

"Done."

My eyes searched his. He was serious. "I was kidding, Mylos."

"If money is what you need, I can give it to you."

I'd never thought about whether he was wealthy. It hadn't mattered. His parents' house in London was lovely but modest.

He nuzzled my neck. "Tell me what's been going on, Pia. All of it. Whatever burdens you've carried on your shoulders, I want to take."

"Why?" It seemed a silly question, but I wanted to know. Why would he take on the struggles of a place where he'd spent little time, for a woman with whom he'd spent little time?

He took a deep breath and cupped my cheek with his palm. "I haven't done a very good job telling you how much you mean to me. That's going to change."

He brought his lips to mine, and I didn't hesitate. I put my arms around his neck and kissed him. He was gentle; I was not. I wanted this man with the same passion I always did.

I stood and held out my hand. When he took it, I led him inside and up the stairs. I saw the bed was unmade in the room he'd stayed in years before. I stepped inside and lifted my sweater over my head.

Mylos unfastened my bra and then my pants. He knelt before me and slid them and my panties off my body. As I stood before him naked, he rested his cheek against my stomach.

"Is this…safe?" he asked.

I nodded, took a step back, sat on the edge of the bed, and watched the beautiful man remove his clothing. He felt self-conscious about his scars, but they didn't bother me. They were part of him, and I loved him. Every part.

I rested against the pillows and spread my legs. Mylos knelt between them. He kissed his way from my pelvic bone up my torso. When he licked my nipples, I squirmed.

"Ticklish?" he asked.

"They ache."

He swirled his tongue around them both and then continued his journey from my neck to my mouth. I grabbed his butt with my hands and pulled him against me.

"Impatient," he teased.

"Always."

We stayed wrapped in each other's arms all morning. Finally, our mutual hunger for food overcame the endless hunger we had for each other.

"I should go to the winery," I said, while we ate the food I'd brought with me earlier that morning.

"Can I come with you?"

"Um…okay."

"Are you hesitant?" he asked.

"Georgio, the winemaker, can be…difficult."

"It's better for him to know I'm here and accept it." Mylos took my hand and brought it to his lips. "I promise not to make things more difficult between you and him, but I won't hide, Pia. It's important that everyone here knows I intend to stay and be a part of your life—that includes Valentini."

"My mamma," I gasped, realizing that no one knew where I was, including Lucia and Gabriella. I'd gotten up before anyone else and came straight to the farmhouse after getting food from our kitchen.

"Why don't we go and say hello to her before we go to the winery?"

"Okay."

Mylos brought my hand to his lips a second time, turned it over, and kissed my palm. "What's worrying you?"

"My mother hasn't been well. She's going to wonder why you're here."

"Can we tell her the truth?"

Which truth was that? That he was here because I was pregnant? That we'd secretly been seeing each other for several years? I had no idea how to explain to my mamma why I'd never shared my relationship with Mylos with her. When he asked about saying hello to her, it suddenly occurred to me that my lies of omission may hurt her. Mylos' family knew all about me. Mine knew nothing about him. Maybe he would be hurt too, that I'd kept him a secret.

"I haven't told her about the baby."

"Pia, I know you're worried, but I promise you, everything will be okay."

"How can you be sure?"

"She'll want you to be happy. That's all that will matter to her."

I smiled. He was right.

Since the day was as warm as yesterday, we took our time walking up the hill to the house. As we passed, many of the workers who were in the vineyards, checking to see if the vines were ready for pruning, tipped their hats or waved.

"I remember the first time I was here, they used to make fun of me."

I laughed. "What are you talking about?"

"They knew I was arse over elbows for you, and they got a kick out of it."

"Arse over elbows?"

"Head over heels? Crazy in love?"

I stopped walking. "Crazy in love?"

Mylos cupped my cheek with his palm like he had earlier. "From the first time I saw you."

I looked away. "A teenage crush."

He rested his forehead against mine. "No, Pia. Love."

I shook my head. "How can you say you love me? You hardly know me."

"I know that isn't what you really believe."

"What do you mean?"

"You've always known how I feel about you in the same way I've known how you feel about me."

We kept walking, and when we arrived at the house, I saw my mamma sitting on the *terrazza*.

"Buongiorno," she said, waving and not looking at all surprised that Mylos was with me.

"Mamma, this is Mylos—"

She stood and rushed over to him, kissing his cheeks. She said something to him that I couldn't hear, and he smiled.

"Have you eaten?" she asked at the same time Lucia joined us.

"We had pastries and fruit," I told them.

A look passed between my mother and Lucia. Both of their eyes were suddenly hooded.

"What's wrong?"

My mamma shook her head. "Nothing, sweetheart."

She was lying. "Is there a problem with my eating the food from my own kitchen, Mamma?"

"Of course there isn't."

"Then, explain."

"In your condition, I—"

"Wait. In my condition?"

My mother led me to the table and pulled out a chair. "Sit, Pia."

I glared at her. "I'm not a dog."

She looked over at Mylos, shrugged, and smiled. "Sit anyway."

My cheeks burned in embarrassment, but I sat down.

My mother sat in front of me and took my hands in hers. "I know you're pregnant."

I nodded, not wanting to ask how in front of Mylos or Lucia.

"Next, I do look through the mail from time to time, Pia. I've known you and Mylos were corresponding for years."

I wished my mother and I were having this conversation without an audience. As it was, I was at a loss for words.

"What I was going to say earlier is, in your condition, I want you to be careful what you're eating."

"I am careful, Mamma."

Again, her eyes met Lucia's. This time, I knew better than to ask why.

"How are you managing?" Mylos asked as we walked from the house to the winery.

"Feeling a bit like you get with Lily sometimes."

He threw his head back and laughed. "I'm sorry, but I know exactly what you mean. You should know it happens with my mum and dad too."

By the time we reached the office, I felt fatigued. The last thing I had energy for was an argument with Georgio. Given Mylos' presence, it was inevitable.

"Let's skip the winery today."

"If that's what you'd like to do."

"I've gotten used to napping in the afternoon. Is that terrible?"

"Sounds bloody brilliant to me."

Little by little, I moved more of the things I needed daily down to the farmhouse. I also spent less and less time in the winery offices. That didn't mean I wasn't working.

When I took over operations after my father's death, I automated so many of the things we did manually that I could handle most of the administrative tasks without a staff. Now, I just took it a step further and worked remotely from the farmhouse.

Mylos and I began most days in the village where we'd buy food that we'd prepare together. When we returned to Valentini, I would work for a few hours, and then in the afternoon, we would read pregnancy books together and then nap—usually preceded by making love.

Before we fell asleep the night before, we agreed that today we'd discuss Valentini and the struggles I was having. It had been easy to avoid thinking about them during the holidays, but it was becoming imperative that I make drastic changes or consider selling. I didn't want to do either.

I began by recounting some of the things that had happened at the winery in the last few years—the theft; the equipment failures, including the one that resulted in our former winemaker almost dying; and my father's accident. I also told him about the most recent issues, like the corking machine failing and the distributor from London canceling their order citing quality issues.

"What happened?"

"I suspect Paolo may have something to do with it."

"Was there ever an investigation into your father's accident?"

"Yes, but the local police didn't get anywhere." I shook my head.

"What?"

"I don't think they tried very hard. I felt the same way about the thefts. I still don't understand how they couldn't have any suspects. That wine only had value if it was sold."

Mylos nodded. "What about the ventilation failure? Was that ever investigated?"

"No. I mean, it was the equipment."

"How is the former winemaker, by the way?"

"Elio?" He was a winemaker from days gone by. The reason Georgio had always spoken with my father about modernization was because Elio fought against it intransigently. I wondered now if it had been a mistake not to continue to do things his way after he left.

"I can see the ideas spinning. Tell me what you're thinking, beautiful."

"It would be nice to pay a visit to Elio and Nonna Carina."

"Nonna Carina?"

"Lucia's mother. They're her parents. I'd like to see how they are."

I'd also like to pay a visit to Nonna Bella for the same reason; however, I had no idea where in the village her sister lived, and with every attempt I'd made to find out, I hit a wall.

22

Grinder

After our visit to Valentini's former winemaker and his wife, Pia's spirits were buoyed. They'd reminisced about her father, and Elio told stories about her being underfoot in the winery when she was a little girl.

At one point, when Pia excused herself to the loo—something pregnant women had to do with great frequency, I was told—I asked Mr. Cesare if he missed working.

"There have been many times I thought about going back." He shook his head, and the look on his face darkened. "Georgio Rossi. I will dance on his grave," he spat.

He made no further mention of it when Pia returned, but I found it curious.

Many of the things she'd told me plagued the winery continued to bother me. The theft, her father's accident, even the ventilation equipment failure. Taking all of that into consideration along with the loss of wine when the cooling systems went out and, finally, the loss of the order from the English distributor, it seemed more than a streak of bad luck.

I found the winemaker's vehement comment about Georgio troubling too.

My gut was telling me there was far more to this story than met the eye. I had every intention of getting to the bottom of it.

In the days that followed, Pia and I walked the grounds and vineyards of Valentini. Each time, I was struck by the contrast between the farmhouse and the newer villa.

"When was that built?" I asked one day, pointing to the sandstone structure that looked almost like a monastery—magnificent in its immense simplicity.

"In the mid-seventeen hundreds, by my seventh great-grandmother, Estancia."

"I thought it was newer."

Pia shrugged and followed my gaze. "It's timeless, I suppose, but then, most Italian architecture is."

Like many other villas I'd seen, this one was comprised of three stories. The main level, as in most, was where the sitting rooms, dining rooms, and kitchen were located. The bedrooms, bathrooms, and lounges were on the second floor, and the third was typically reserved for storage as well as a dormitory for the servants.

I hadn't been on the second or third floors of this particular villa, but the first had spacious rooms with high ceilings and big windows, offering stunning panoramic views of the estate. Lavish weavings done in an array of colors hung on the light-colored stone walls, giving the place a warmth so unlike homes in England.

There were more outbuildings on the property than I realized. Many small cottages sat empty and could easily be renovated to serve as guest accommodations. All it would take was money. We hadn't circled back to that conversation, but I intended to soon.

I couldn't say for certain she felt the same way I did, but her fear of me finding "real Pia" less attractive than "dream Pia" was unfounded. I enjoyed every minute I spent with her. My goal of relieving her stress had resulted in lowering mine.

She'd all but taken up residence in the farmhouse; however, she'd insisted we move to the room with the bigger bed. I was already envisioning making one of the smaller rooms into a nursery like Lily and Wills had done in their house. Not that I'd mentioned that to Pia.

While I was ready to plan out the rest of our lives, something inside said to take it slower with Pia. I'd promised her that, with every sunrise and sunset, she'd see she could believe in me. I was in no hurry, since I had no plans to go anywhere. I did, however, intend to bring a couple of people here.

The next afternoon, while Pia napped, I had two calls to make. The first was to Decker.

"I have a few people I need to look into," I told him when he answered.

"Shoot."

I gave him three names to start. Paolo Viticcio, Georgio Rossi, and Mateo Casavetti.

"Anything else?"

"Not yet."

"I'll call ya back."

While I didn't think it would take him long, I doubted he had any information when my mobile rang with a call from him a few minutes later.

"You sure as hell have gotten yourself in the middle of a hornet's nest, Grinder."

I scrubbed my face with my hand. "That didn't take long."

"It doesn't when there's an ongoing investigation being conducted by an international intelligence agency."

"Which one?"

"The AISE, aka the Italian CIA."

I was familiar with the acronym for the Agenzia Informazioni e Sicurezza Esterna. "What are they investigating?"

"If you aren't sitting down, you better."

"Go on."

"Murder linked to Italian royalty. They take that shit pretty serious over there."

"Who?"

"Giovanni Deltetto."

"Not a heart attack?"

"No, it was, but brought on by poisoning."

"Bloody hell."

"That isn't all. I haven't found how this relates yet, but the Valentini name came up in an AISE investigation into ancient antiquities that have been turning up on the black market."

Deck was right about me landing in the middle of a hornet's nest. Worse was the idea that Pia was living in it.

"As far as your background information, I've only got the goods on two so far. Actually, only one you asked about. Mateo Casavetti is a mid-level AISE agent. The second is Lucia Cesare, she's a rung below him and currently undercover at the Valentini estate. Since they both had ties to the family, there was no need for assumed identities."

Lucia? I didn't see that one coming. Although, the report on Pia's cousin Mateo surprised me just as much.

"I'll get back to you when I know something more. Also, you might want to think about putting a team together on this, Grind. Somethin' tells me that the deeper I go, the worse what I have to tell you will be."

"Thanks, mate. My next call was going to be to Rile anyway."

"Let me know who's on your wish list, and I'll see if I can get their twenty."

"Got it. And, Deck, I understand this better than you know, but you need to stay in Texas with Mila."

"That was cryptic."

I took a deep breath. This would be the first I revealed this news to anyone. "Pia is pregnant."

"You okay about this?"

"Yes. As a matter of fact, I'm somewhat over the moon."

"I'm happy for you, Grinder. I mean that sincerely. It's a hell of a thing to watch the woman you love, growing your baby inside of her." He cleared his throat. "That's if you love her, I guess."

"I do, Decker, and you're right. It is a hell of a thing."

"By the way, Rile's in Madrid, and I can tell you, he isn't happy."

"So he'd welcome a mission, then?"

"Like you wouldn't believe."

I rang Rile as soon as Deck ended our call. "I may need your assistance."

"Yeah? What have you got?"

"Death of Italian royalty. An AISE investigation into ancient antiquities being sold on the black market. You in?"

"Damn straight."

I almost laughed out loud at how much Rile sounded like Decker with that response.

"Decker hasn't been able to find out what one has to do with the other, but he's working on it."

Rile offered to contact Z to see what MI6 knew, as well as "round up" some support on our end. I couldn't help but take the piss out of him for how much he sounded like a cowboy.

"I need to stay the hell outta Texas," he muttered before he rang off.

The next morning, I received a message from Decker, asking me to check in with him as soon as possible.

"Viticcio is person of interest *numero uno* in Deltetto's murder, as well as a primary suspect in the black market antiquities ring. I haven't figured out what Rossi's role is. He may just be Viticcio's lackey. Oh, and there's a third, a woman, Donnatella Bianchi."

"Any idea who they're working for?"

"Not sure there is anyone else. While the value of what they're selling is astronomical, there hasn't been a whole hell of a lot of it. Quality over quantity, I guess. Oh, and from what I read, Viticcio has been sniffing around Valentini for years."

"Sniffing around for what?"

"You aren't going to believe this."

"Go on."

"The ancient consular route Via Cassia passed through Val d'Orcia—right past *Antica Cascina dei Conti di Valentini,* specifically."

I didn't want to take the wind from Deck's sails, but this was hardly news. "Any tourist guide in Tuscany could tell you that."

"I bet they couldn't tell you who passed through on that route more than a thousand years later."

"Who, Decker?"

"The Sovereign Order of Malta."

"What is that?"

"Who."

"Right. Who?"

"You've heard of the Knights Templar?"

"Of course."

"The Malta Sovereigns are said to have buried ten times the treasures of the Templars."

"Are you suggesting there's a treasure buried somewhere on the Valentini estate?"

"It's very likely. I was able to access an archive with some interesting information about Pia's ancestors. Estancia Valentini, in particular. What I've read says she agreed to give the Italian government half of the value of the Valentini fortune in exchange for control of her own estate. I guess she had 'em over a barrel, since they altered the inheritance laws regarding her property—and hers alone."

I could hear him typing on a keyboard in the background. "There's more. This was a side note, but important enough that someone added it. Anyone who attempted to change or alter her wishes would be cursed for all eternity."

"And they believed her?"

"Like I said, enough to make mention of it. Supposedly, it all started with her husband. The archives say he tried to get control of her estate and leave it to his sons from a previous marriage. You don't want to know what happened to him."

"What happened?"

"I just told you that you don't want to know. I'm not fuckin' around here, Grinder."

"Understood. What archive did you hack into, Decker?"

"You don't want to know that either, man."

"How deep was this buried?"

"Way, way deep. Back in the late seventeen hundreds, when this all went down, there were rampant rumors about this alleged buried treasure, but they were squashed. It wasn't long after Estancia made her deal with the government. Could be they covered the rest of it up as part of their agreement."

"Say there was a treasure buried somewhere on Valentini. Who would it belong to?"

"Because of the deal I just mentioned, it belongs to the owner of the estate."

"Pia's mother?"

"That's right. However, it doesn't mean it can't be stolen."

"You think this is what Viticcio is after?"

"Think about it, Grinder. Estancia Valentini gave the Italian government half. Can you imagine what the other half would be worth now?"

"You were able to find this rather quickly, Deck. Couldn't someone else do the same?"

"Just in case you left your brain in London, do you have any idea who you're talking to?"

"Right. Sorry. I'm a wanker."

"You got that right."

23

I took a deep breath and opened the door to the winery office. Mylos said he had a few calls to make, so I decided it was time to inform Georgio of his presence and get it over with.

I looked around the space that had bustled with people when I was growing up. It was still and quiet now.

The winery itself was a different story. Georgio managed over a hundred employees. During the harvest and bottling, that number jumped significantly.

One of the things I'd picked up on recently was that his labor costs were high for this time of year. It was something I knew would lead to an argument, but it was a conversation we had to have.

I heard the office door open and turned to see Mylos walk in.

"Did you finish your calls?"

"Yes." He put his hands on my shoulders. "You're tense."

"Thinking about having a conversation with Georgio does that."

He continued rubbing my shoulders but didn't comment.

"Aren't you going to tell me to fire him?"

He leaned forward so his mouth was close to my ear. "I will never tell you to do anything…in regard to the winery."

I looked over my shoulder and smiled. "Had to get that caveat in, yes?"

As he kissed me, I heard the door leading to the production area open. Every muscle in my body went on high alert, knowing it was Georgio.

"Hello," I heard Mylos say as he walked toward him. When he held out his hand, Georgio hesitated, but did shake it.

"Miles—Mylos—Stone," he said.

"Georgio Rossi," he grunted.

I picked up the labor cost report. "I asked you to meet me so we could discuss labor costs." I handed it to him.

"When?"

I cocked my head. "Now."

He looked over at Mylos, who pulled a chair out from one of the desks and sat down.

"We'll do this later." Georgio dropped the paper and turned to walk out.

"We'll do this now, Georgio. Right now."

He spun around, looking from me to Mylos. "Excuse us."

"He stays."

Georgio's eyes scrunched.

"He stays, Georgio."

He picked up the report and waved it at me. "What about this?"

"The numbers are high for this time of year."

"They're not."

"Look at the yearly comparison. Particularly in manual labor. What is the explanation for the difference?"

"Your numbers are wrong."

He'd spoken to me disrespectfully one too many times, and while I had to admit that Mylos' presence gave me courage I might not otherwise have had, the decision I made was mine alone.

"You have three choices, Georgio. You can explain why the numbers are so out of proportion; you can accept a demotion and relinquish your role as head winemaker; or you can resign, effective immediately."

Georgio's face turned bright red. When he stepped closer, Mylos got up and stood beside me.

"You are making a big mistake," he seethed, looking first at Mylos and then at me.

"I have made mistakes, Georgio. The biggest one is failing to remind you that you work for me, not the other way around."

"You can't fire me."

"I can. So if you're not prepared to explain the cost overages, I'll do just that."

His mouth hung open. "You're not serious."

"I'm very serious."

His eyes darted between Mylos and me. "You're finished. You know that, right? You'll drive the final nail in Valentini's coffin."

"Actually, I intend to remove some that you have driven in yourself."

Georgio stepped closer still.

"Watch it," warned Mylos.

"I'll give you some time to put a report together, explaining the cost overages. We'll meet back here tomorrow."

Georgio stormed out.

"You okay?" Mylos asked.

"Yes. It's been a long time since I've felt as okay as I do now. I have you to thank."

"You handled that all on your own, Pia."

"I need to discuss this with my mother."

Mylos looked as if he was about to say something, but only nodded.

We walked up to the house hand in hand. My mamma wasn't on the *terrazza*, but it was chillier today. Perhaps she was having her morning meal in the sitting room. When we went inside, she wasn't there either.

I saw Lucia coming down the stairs.

"Have you seen the countess?"

"She's not feeling well. She's still in bed."

"Go ahead," said Mylos. "I'll chat with Lucia for a minute and then come up."

I wanted to ask what about, but if he'd wanted me to know, I suppose he would've said.

I knocked on my mother's bedroom door. "It's me, Mamma," I said when I didn't hear a response. I opened the door and found her in bed with the sheets pulled up to her chin. She looked over at me and motioned me closer. "Lucia said you were feeling poorly."

"*Sì.* Come closer."

I sat beside her on the bed.

"What is bothering you, sweetheart?"

"For one, I'm worried about you."

She reached out from under the bedclothes and patted my hand. "I'll be okay. I sense there's something else, though."

We heard a knock at the door. "Who is it?" I called out.

"Lucia."

"She's bringing me some tea. Open the door."

When I did, she walked in, carrying a tray. "I thought you might like to try to eat something."

When my mother thanked her, I waited for Lucia to leave, but she didn't.

"What were we talking about?" my mamma asked.

"It's about Georgio."

She took a sip of tea and looked over at Lucia, who again, didn't leave. "What about him?"

"I want to let him go."

"Why?" Both women's eyes opened wide.

"Because he's insolent and disrespectful." The door creaked open, and Mylos stuck his head in. "Sorry to interrupt. Lucia asked me to join you when I finished my phone call."

"Come in," said my mother. "Go on, Pia, about Georgio."

"He argues with me about everything. This morning, I asked him to explain what I saw as labor cost overages, and he refused."

"I see."

This was not the reaction I expected from my mother. "I'm tired of it, Mamma."

"You haven't mentioned this to Paolo, have you?"

"Paolo? Why would I?" I was beginning to get angry.

"What about Mateo? It might be helpful to get his opinion."

"Would you have said the same to Papà?"

"I'm only suggesting it might be helpful to discuss it with him. If you were to let him go, who would replace him?"

"Elio Cesare," I answered without hesitation, looking over at Lucia.

Again, my mother's eyes opened wide. "Elio?"

"Yes. Mylos and I went to visit him. I got the impression he would love to come back as long as Georgio was no longer here."

"That's an interesting proposal, but…"

"But I should discuss it with Mateo," I said when my mother didn't finish her sentence.

"*Sì.*"

I stood and left the room, knowing that if I didn't, my temper would cause me to say things to my mother that I might regret. This was so unlike her. Whenever I discussed matters such as this with her before, she'd always said it was my decision. Why not now? Also, why hadn't Lucia said anything? She had to know as well as I did that her father would want to come back.

"Do you agree?" I asked Mylos when he followed me downstairs.

"Only in that it might be worth getting his opinion. It's still up to you to weigh what he has to say against your intuition."

I huffed and folded my arms.

Mylos smiled and unfolded them. "What was that about?"

"So logical."

He kissed my cheek. "One phone call and then make your decision."

It wasn't that easy. Mateo encouraged me to hold off. When I asked why, he was vague but reiterated he thought I should wait.

I didn't like it, but given he and my mother felt so strongly, I decided to give it more time. If Georgio persisted in his disrespectful treatment of me, I'd do what I thought best.

When I left the winery office, I found Mylos outside, talking to Lucia. She stopped mid-sentence when she saw me. "Go on," I said.

"We were just talking about your mother not feeling well."

I didn't believe her. If that were the case, she'd have no reason to end their conversation because of me. Something else occurred to me.

"Why did you bring Mamma her breakfast today instead of Gabriella?"

"I usually do, just to make it easier."

"Don't you have work of your own to do?"

Both she and Mylos appeared stunned at my tone. I didn't care. I sensed they were hiding something, and it angered me.

"*Mi scusi,*" she muttered and went inside.

"Pia?"

I walked over to the railing and looked out over the vineyard. "What were you talking about?" I waited, knowing that if he lied to me, we were finished. There were too many people in my life I couldn't trust.

"There is a lot I need to tell you, but this isn't the time nor the place."

I let out the breath I didn't realize I was holding.

"When and where?"

He walked over and took my hand. "Now. The farmhouse."

I almost wept in relief. It would've broken my heart if he hadn't responded the way he did.

24

Grinder

As we walked down the hill from the villa, I thought a great deal about what I should and shouldn't tell Pia.

Many things were happening behind the scenes of her life, more than I'd thought, based on my conversations with Lucia this morning and my follow-up call with Decker.

Part of it needed to stay in place for the time being—mainly regarding Georgio and the fill-in cook, Gabriella—and neither could suspect anything was out of the ordinary. Could Pia pull it off? I wasn't certain. Her life depended on her being so. But could she trust me if I didn't tell her everything?

Instead of going inside when we reached the farmhouse, I led Pia to the *terrazza*. Once she was seated, I moved a chair over and sat in front of her.

"There are things I can tell you now and other things that would be best if I didn't."

She slowly nodded her head.

"I need you to tell me if you can be okay with that."

"I don't know."

That was fair, and I said so.

"You're frightening me."

"There is danger in regard to what I'm about to tell you, Pia. I won't hide that from you."

She gripped my hands with sweaty palms.

"The struggles you've been experiencing have not been mere accidents," I began. "They happened systematically in an effort to make one of two things happen. First, that you would turn to Paolo Viticcio, perhaps even agree to marry him. Barring that, the second would be that you would agree to sell Valentini. There is reason to believe Georgio is involved as well."

"Why?"

"Valentini may be worth far more than the vineyards and wine."

"Estancia's fortune."

Her response surprised me. Perhaps she knew more than anyone realized. "Yes."

"They're attempting to get control of Valentini over something that may not even exist? That makes no sense."

"There are reasons to believe it does exist, Pia."

"What?"

"It's possible they found proof."

I watched as she processed what I'd just told her.

"How is Lucia involved?"

"It would be best if you didn't know at this time." I felt her stiffen. "Pia, trust me. I know it's difficult, but I promise that whatever information I keep from you is only to ensure your safety."

"Why isn't it as simple as barring them from Valentini?" The moment the words left her mouth, she turned white. "Did they have something to do with my father's death?"

I couldn't just hold her hands. I needed to soothe her. I pulled her from the chair and onto my lap. "Yes, Pia. Your father's heart attack may have been brought on by something else."

"They killed him?"

"There is a strong belief that was the case."

"Mio Dio." Pia covered her mouth with her hand and raced into the farmhouse. I followed her to the lavatory and rubbed her back as she emptied the contents of her stomach. I knew then that I'd gone too far. There was no way she'd be able to feign ignorance in front of Georgio. In fact, I feared she'd go after him.

I helped her to a chair in the sitting room and took out my mobile.

"We need to talk. We'll come to you," I said when Lucia answered. "Where are Georgio and Gabriella?"

"Gabriella?" Pia mouthed, and I nodded.

"I don't know," Lucia answered, "but I'll find them. Tell Pia to come into the main house from the back way."

"Do you feel well enough to return to the villa?"

"Yes."

I heard a vehicle drive up to the farmhouse and stood to see who it was. Rile's timing could not have been better, nor could his choice of a black SUV with darkly tinted windows.

"Hello, my friend," he said when I opened the door. "This must be the lovely Pia." He took her outstretched hand, brought it to his lips, and kissed the back of it.

"Pia, this is Cortez DeLéon, also known as Rile. He is one of my business partners."

She appeared wary, and rightly so. Her world had just been rocked significantly. I could only imagine the gamut of her emotions.

"We were about to go up to the main house. A ride would be helpful."

Rile nodded and led the way.

"A moment," said Pia, going back to the lavatory. "I'll be right out."

"I'll be waiting," I murmured as she closed the door behind her.

When the door opened, her breath smelled of mint but her hand was on her tummy. "Feeling better or should we wait?"

"Better."

"Lucia mentioned a back way into the house," I said as we approached the villa.

"That way," Pia said, pointing left. "Stop here."

I didn't see anything that looked like a way in, but followed her around a corner and down some stone steps while Rile waited in the SUV. "What is this?" I asked when we came to what looked like an ancient door that had rarely been used.

"It leads to the cellar, where there is another set of stairs that go back up."

The secret staircase took us to the second floor and Countess Maria's bedroom.

We knocked and entered when Pia's mother called out to us to do so. The moment the door closed behind us, she threw back the bedclothes. Underneath, she was fully dressed.

"I'm sorry, Pia. We wanted to tell you before now, but there didn't seem to be a good time."

"You are well, Mamma?" she murmured, holding tightly to my hand.

"*Sì.* Lucia is the one who figured it out."

"Figured out what?"

Lucia looked at me, and I nodded. While I didn't want to divulge this information yet, Pia would see my refusal as hiding something everyone else seemed to know.

"You and your mother were being poisoned," Lucia told her.

"*What?*"

"Sit down, Pia." Her mother patted the bed next to her. "In your condition, you shouldn't be under a lot of stress."

Pia didn't budge. "I'm aware of that, Mamma. However, sitting down will not do a thing to alleviate it."

It was time for me to take over the conversation, and I did, telling the other people in the room the same things I'd told Pia earlier. When finished, I turned to her.

"Given all of that, I think it would be best if you left Valentini temporarily."

"I spoke with Mateo. He suggested that she and Countess Maria go to Casavetti," said Lucia.

"It's a viable solution," I said when Pia looked up at me.

"For how long?"

That, I couldn't answer and said so.

"No."

25

Pia

I had no intention of leaving my home, now or ever. I certainly wouldn't be forced out by the likes of Paolo and Georgio. However, I didn't feel comfortable continuing this conversation in my mother's bedroom.

"Lucia, you take Mamma down the back staircase. There's someone waiting there who will drive you to the farmhouse. Mylos and I will walk."

We were halfway there when I noticed he was smiling.

"What?"

"I should've known you'd react this way."

"Which way?"

"That you'd face what's happening at Valentini head-on." When he stopped walking, I did too. "I'm sorry I doubted you, Pia."

"What did you think I would do?"

"Go after Georgio. Maybe claw his eyes out."

I laughed, and so did he. "I want to, believe me, but first, I have questions."

Once at the farmhouse, I sat down on the sofa, next to my mother. She put her hand on my shoulder and stroked my hair.

"I'm so sorry we didn't realize what was happening in time to save your papà. I am sad every day, thinking of my beloved husband."

"I'm sorry, Mamma."

She nodded. "Soon, this will all be over."

Lucia, sitting on the other side of the room, nodded. "It will be. Very soon."

"How did you know someone was trying to poison us?" I asked her.

She looked at Mylos, who nodded.

"First, we found out that was what killed your father. He had a heart attack, but it was a result of the poison."

"Who poisoned him?"

Lucia looked at Mylos again. He nodded a second time.

"Stop doing that!" I shouted. *"Don't ask him what you can tell me. Just tell me."* I clenched my fists when she did it a third time.

"I'm sorry, Pia."

"Just tell me," I growled.

"We believe it was Georgio. Once Gabriella arrived, we think she's been the one attempting to poison you and your mother."

"Were you ever really ill, Mamma?"

"*Sì*, but only for a very short time."

"Lucia…" I rubbed my stomach. I couldn't say the words.

"That's why I've been at the house, Pia. I've been intercepting your food and that of your mother's. You and the baby are fine."

That was why she and my mother had acted so strangely when I took food from our kitchen down to the farmhouse.

"Who do you work for?" When she looked at Mylos once more, I wanted to jump up and slap her.

"I am an agent with the *Agenzia Informazioni e Sicurezza Esterna.*"

"And that is why you've been filling in for your mother?"

"Yes."

"What about Mateo? Is he really your boyfriend?"

"I'm sorry, Pia. Everything we've done has been to protect you."

"Answer me."

"He is, but he also works for AISE."

"If you know that Georgio killed my father, why haven't you arrested him?" When Lucia looked at Mylos again, I wanted to scream.

"I'll answer that," he said. "There isn't sufficient evidence." He rubbed the back of his neck with his hand. "There is also the matter of certain antiquities being offered for sale on the black market."

"Paolo?"

"He's a suspect, yes."

"What about Georgio's cousin, Gabriella? What role does she play, other than trying to murder my mamma and me?"

Before anyone could answer, there was a knock at the door. I gasped and put my hand over my heart.

"Don't worry, Rile is outside." When Mylos opened the door, Mateo walked in.

He came straight over to my mamma. "Don't get up," he said and then cheek-kissed her.

"Hi, Pia." He did the same to me.

"I contacted Mateo to let him know you'd decided to remain at Valentini. I suggested it might be best if he came here and briefed us on the status of AISE's investigation."

Mateo cleared his throat and remained standing while Mylos took a seat next to me.

"Go ahead," he told him.

"Approximately six years ago, AISE received intel about a group of individuals who were systematically targeting historic estates, particularly those found along the ancient Roman road Via Cassia. In most cases, the estates had fallen into disrepair and the owners were anxious to sell. This group, whose identities are shrouded in a dummy corporation, were willing buyers.

"AISE got involved when first, it appeared they were using more heavy-handed means to get reluctant owners to sell. In particular, Valentini. Second, when rare antiquities began appearing on the black market."

When no one had any comments or questions, Mateo continued. He looked directly at me. "The failing equipment and thefts at Valentini were suspicious, but when your father suffered an injury more than likely intended to take his life, we stepped up our efforts. Given my close relationship with your family, I was chosen to go undercover, as was Lucia."

I didn't like their subterfuge, but what choice had they had? If it weren't for them, my mamma and I might be dead.

"Your father's trust in Paolo Viticcio ended up working to our benefit, at least initially, given we were able to monitor his actions. What we didn't realize until it was too late, was that after the accident didn't kill him, your father was slowly being poisoned to death."

Mateo looked at Lucia. It wasn't accusatory; it was more sympathetic. No doubt she blamed herself for not figuring it out sooner.

"It was only after we sent some of your food to the lab that we realized it was being poisoned with mercury."

My mother was slowly nodding her head. It appeared she already knew most of what Mateo was saying.

"What about Nonna Bella?"

Mateo looked at Lucia a second time. "We have no reason to believe she was aware of what was happening," she answered. "Nor was my mother."

"Before you arrived, I asked about Georgio's cousin, Gabriella."

"She isn't his cousin," Mateo answered. "Her real name is Donnatella Bianchi, and we believe that she and Paolo may be the masterminds in this conspiracy—"

"Donnatella?" I closed my eyes, picturing the woman I met in the lobby of the hotel in London and then the woman who became our fill-in cook. Without makeup and with the addition of frumpy clothes, flat shoes instead of heels, her hair dyed or wearing a wig, and a pair of glasses, they could be the same person.

It explained so much. Including why Mylos had seen him leave with a "beautiful blonde" the night Paolo and I had dinner with the Fellwood partners. Now I wondered if they were in on it too.

I reached for Mylos' hand. I felt as though he and my mother were the only people in my life who weren't pretending to be someone else, but I had to be sure. I turned and looked into his eyes. "How long have you known about this?"

"A few days. Once you shared the details of Valentini's struggles, I grew suspicious and asked another of my partners to do some research."

I looked up at Mateo. "Have any of these antiquities been proven to have come from the Via Cassia estates?"

He shook his head. "Since there is little proof the buried treasures, for lack of a better term, existed, it is impossible to say. However, research is currently being done to determine the age of what's being sold."

"What do we do now?"

Rather than answer, Mateo looked at Mylos.

"Why are you looking at him? Why is he looking at you?" I shouted.

I heard the front door open and gasped like I had when we heard the knock.

"Excuse me," said the man Mylos had introduced as Rile. "May I?"

Since he was looking at me, I nodded.

Mylos stood and held his hand out to me; I followed them through the kitchen and out to the *terrazza*. "I may be better able to explain," he said once I was seated.

"You heard our conversation?"

"I should have told you," Mylos said, taking my hand in his. "I allowed Rile to listen in."

"Okay." I took several deep breaths and let each one out slowly.

"I know that *Mylos* has told you I am one of his business partners."

"Yes."

"Do you know the nature of that business?"

"No."

"We provide private security and intelligence for our clients."

"Am I one of your clients?" I asked, looking from him to Mylos and back again.

Rile smiled. "And our families. The collective background of our partners allows us to use different means to find information than, say, a government agency would be able to use." He waited for me to nod that I understood. "This is why your cousin looked to Mylos rather than answer himself."

Now I understood why Mateo had been so cautious in front of Mylos, and also why this man, Rile, suggested we come outside. "Then, I'll ask you. What do we do now?"

"We force them to act, and when they do, we catch them."

"How do we do that?"

Rile sat back and brushed his lower lip with his index finger, all the while staring at Mylos.

Finally, he spoke. "You get married."

"What? No!"

Mylos squeezed my hand and laughed. "Is the idea of marrying me really that horrible?"

"You could marry me instead if you'd prefer." Rile winked, and Mylos made a sound like a growling animal.

"What does my marrying achieve?"

"Part of it would be to 'leak' information regarding your future husband's financial status along with his intention to invest a great deal of his fortune into the Valentini estate," Rile answered.

"Remember, I told you earlier the struggles you've been experiencing weren't accidents. They happened systematically in an effort to make you agree to marry Paolo or agree to sell Valentini."

"Yes. So, if I make Paolo believe I'm going to marry you, and you have money, he will see that he has no chance to purchase Valentini."

"That's right."

"At this point, I'd like to bring one of our other partners in on the conversation," said Rile, who tapped the screen of his cell phone.

"Hello, Pia, I'm Decker," said the man Rile put on speakerphone.

"Hello," I responded.

"I'd hoped you could share any additional information you may have on the antiquities investigation," Rile prompted.

"Sure. I've been looking into the purchase records for the various estates located on the ancient consular route Via Cassia."

"And?" Mylos asked.

"There's a definite method to their madness."

"What are you saying, Deck?"

"They know in advance which estates they want, almost as if they have a map."

"A map?" I gasped as memories began flooding my brain.

"Hold on, Decker," I heard Mylos say. He put his arm around my shoulders. "Talk to me, sweetheart."

"When we were kids, Georgio, Lucia, and I used to play hide and seek in the wine caves. One day we found this old chest, like you see in the movies. It was half-buried behind a rack of ancient wine barrels. We convinced each other we'd found a secret treasure, but all we found were rolled-up old papers." Another image flashed in my mind. Was my memory playing tricks on me, or had I just figured out how Paolo knew which estates to target? "I need to speak with Lucia."

She had been there that day too. Would she recollect the same things I did?

"Why don't we all go back inside? Stand by, Deck," said Mylos.

"Roger that."

We sat back down on the sofa while Rile explained to my mother, Mateo, and Lucia that, in the midst of our conversation, I remembered something that might be significant.

"Go ahead," Mylos said to me.

I turned toward Lucia. "Remember when we were kids, how you, Georgio, and I used to play in the wine caves?"

"Of course."

"One time we explored a part of the caves where we'd never been before."

"I think I remember."

"We found an old chest and were certain we'd found a secret treasure."

Lucia's face turned pale, and her eyes opened wide.

"Who else was with us that day, Lucia?"

"Paolo," she gasped.

I turned to my mother. "You remember. Papà had invited his parents to visit, and he came with them."

"*Sì,* I remember."

My mind raced. Was that the same day I'd found the red heart-shaped stone?

"Pia?" I heard Mylos say.

"I'm sorry. What?"

"Decker asked if you thought you could find your way back to the chest."

"Maybe…" It had been so long since I was in those caves. I closed my eyes and rubbed my temples with my fingertips.

"Lucia, could you?" Rile asked.

"I'm not sure, but we could try," I heard Lucia answer. "Pia, what's wrong?"

I turned to my mother first and then looked at Lucia and finally at Mylos.

"That was the day I found it," I said, barely above a whisper.

"Found what?" my mother asked.

"This?"

I turned to Mylos, and he held the stone in his hand. My mother reached around me to grab it from him, but I was faster. As I closed my hand tightly around it, all conversation in the room ceased. I wasn't sure anyone was even breathing.

"Give it to me, Pia."

"No, Mamma."

"Pia, please."

"What is its significance?"

She shook her head.

"Tell me, or I'll—"

"It isn't just a stone, Pia."

"What is it?"

My mother shook her head a second time.

"Come, Mamma," I said, standing and holding my hand out to her. I led her out to the *terrazza*.

"Something about this stone causes you great distress. Tell me what it is."

"You shouldn't have given it to Mylos."

"Why not?"

"It's cursed."

My first inclination was to roll my eyes, but given my mother's level of agitation, I refrained. I waited, arms folded again, for her to continue.

"Very well. It is believed to have belonged to the Prince of Venetto, Viano de' Medici, also known as the Black Prince. He and his men stole it from the corpse of the Sultan of Grenada after stabbing him to death. Shortly after that happened, Viano contracted a mysterious disease from which he died less than a month later.

"The stone was passed down through the Medici family, with every recipient dying a violent death or from a mysterious disease. It is said that Estancia's first husband stole the gem, and it was found on his body after his death." My mother shuddered.

"How did he die, Mamma?"

"Pia…"

"We're alone. Just tell me."

"He burned to death."

"Mylos…" I couldn't go on. I covered my mouth with my hand, hoping to stave off being sick to my stomach. Unsuccessful, I ran inside to use the lavatory.

All eyes were on me as I walked back out to the *terrazza*. My mother was still seated in the same place.

"It's my fault—"

"Shh." My mother shook her head. "Let's not speak of it."

When we rejoined the others, I could feel Mylos' eyes on me, but I couldn't bear to look at him. Because of me, because of my gift to him, he'd almost died— more than once. First, from the explosion in Iraq and then the explosion in London. By the grace of God, he hadn't, but I could no longer tempt fate.

My heart was breaking, but I had no choice. I had to end things between us. I could never look Mylos in the eye again, knowing that because I'd given him the cursed stone, he'd suffered unimaginably.

"Pia?"

"I am not feeling well, Mylos. I am going to the villa to lie down." I said all of that without looking him in the eye. He stood, most likely to come with me, but I held up my hand.

"Lucia, would you mind going with me?"

She followed me out the door and closed it behind her.

"Pia, what's wrong?"

When my eyes filled with tears and I shook my head, Lucia put her arm around my shoulders.

"We don't have to talk about it."

"I need to rest." I knew the stress I'd experienced in the last couple of hours was bad for the baby. If nothing else, I'd close the draperies in my bedroom and try to sleep.

We walked up the hill in silence. With every step I took, I tried my hardest to let go of the tension in my body, but every time I thought of Mylos and how he'd almost died because of me, I felt my muscles tighten again.

When we reached the *terrazza*, Lucia went ahead of me to open the front door. I walked over to the railing and looked out over the vineyards of Valentini.

The hair on the back of my neck bristled when I sensed I wasn't alone. I looked over my shoulder and saw Paolo standing in the back corner of the *terrazza,* holding a gun to Lucia's head.

"Hello, Pia," he said with an evil smile.

26

Grinder

It was obvious that whatever Countess Maria told Pia about the stone, had jarred her. Never before had she refused to make eye contact with me.

I was torn between following her and giving her some space. At least she hadn't left alone.

"What did you tell her?" I asked when the countess sat back down beside me.

"The stone has…a history," she began after taking a deep breath. "Some say it's cursed."

"Is that what Pia thinks?" I asked.

She nodded.

"I would disagree. I've always seen it as a talisman."

"What is the stone?" asked Rile. "It's obviously something you've seen before."

"Actually, I hadn't, although I've read a description. Given it is quite unique, there is no doubt it is the same one."

Rile took a seat next to the countess. "Tell us," he urged. "So we understand."

Mateo's phone pinged. *"Cazzo! I just got an SOS from Lucia!"*

I jumped to my feet out of instinct. We raced from the house and climbed into the waiting vehicles. When the countess got into the back of the SUV Rile and I were in, I almost told her to wait at the farmhouse, but if she did, she'd be alone with no one to protect her.

We followed Mateo's vehicle up the hill and parked near the *terrazza*. When we got out, I could see Lucia's crumpled form near the back corner. I raced over ahead of Mateo and breathed a sigh of relief when I found a pulse.

Mateo gathered her in his arms while he examined the wound on her forehead.

"What happened?" she groaned, opening her eyes.

"Looks like someone knocked you out."

"Paolo! He's with Pia!" She wiggled out of Mateo's arms and landed on her feet.

"When you say 'with Pia,' what does that mean?"

She clenched her fists. "He made her take him to the place where she hid the Medici diamond!"

"What are you talking about?"

"Come on, she took him to the caves!" When Lucia ran inside the villa, I followed, and so did Mateo.

"Rile," I called out behind me. "Stay with the countess."

The words had just left my mouth when I saw her move out of his grasp and in our direction.

"You need me to show you the way to get to the tunnels."

"See if you can locate Georgio and the woman!" I shouted to Mateo as I rushed to follow Lucia.

"This way," said the countess once we were inside. She motioned us to a back staircase. We raced down the steps, but instead of stopping at the first floor, we continued going down. I recognized it immediately as where Pia had brought us in earlier.

At the next landing, Lucia tried to open a wooden door. When it wouldn't budge, I stepped around her.

"It's locked from the other side," said the countess. "It's never locked."

That meant we were on the right track. I slammed my shoulder against it. Again, it didn't budge. I hurled my body against it a second time, and it gave in the middle.

"Move," said Rile, pushing me out of the way. "Get back!"

I shielded the countess, and Lucia crouched down when we realized what he was about to do.

A shot from his gun, and the door sprang open.

"Look," said Lucia, pointing to what appeared to be fresh footprints in the dirt on the stone floor.

"Do you have any idea where she'd take him?" Rile asked Lucia.

"Probably back to where she found the red stone."

She led the way through the tunnels and outside to the trail that led to the caves. Rile and I held up our mobiles to provide light.

We were halfway up an incline when the countess stopped. "You go ahead," she said, trying to catch her breath.

"Go on," said Rile. "I'll stay."

I nodded and raced ahead with Lucia. When we reached the top, there was a curve, and beyond it, I saw light.

I stopped when I heard footsteps and peered around the corner. When I saw it was Mateo, I eased into view.

"I saw tracks but stayed in the dirt," he said, pointing to the trail that led from the villa to the cave's entrance. The parted grasses were high, indicating someone had just come that way.

We crept farther back in the caves. I stopped when I thought I heard a scream.

27

Pia

After we walked into the caves, I saw Georgio waiting. I looked into his eyes and shook my head. When he smirked in response, I wanted to claw his eyes out, just like Mylos had predicted.

In hindsight, I wondered if I'd made a mistake in agreeing to lead Paolo to what he was looking for as long as Lucia didn't come with us. It never occurred to me that I'd be outnumbered.

"I told you she'd know where it is."

"Why are you here? I told you to wait in the tunnels," Paolo spat at Georgio.

"And leave you alone with the diamond? Not a chance."

Paolo leaned into me so his mouth was near my ear. "If you're playing me, know that I will kill you." The gun he'd had trained on me the whole way through the tunnels, pressed into my side.

When he pushed me, I kept walking, hoping I'd be able to find the place where we'd discovered the chest all those years ago.

Once I found that, I could probably locate the place where I'd originally picked up the stone I gave to Mylos.

I'd never heard of the Medici diamond and had no idea why Paolo thought I knew where it was, but the only thing I could think of was that maybe it was buried somewhere near where I'd found the other stone.

"This way," I said, rounding a familiar-looking corner.

I recognized the wine racks, but I couldn't see if the chest was still behind them. I stopped and looked around, trying to get my bearings. "There," I said, motioning with my head to an offshoot about twenty feet from where we stood.

Paolo grabbed my arm and jerked me forward. Once we rounded another corner, he pushed me so hard I fell to my knees. I heard a clicking sound and looked over my shoulder, screaming when I saw Georgio fall to the ground. When he landed, I could see blood trickling down from a bullet hole in his forehead.

"You're going to kill me too, aren't you?" I said, looking into Paolo's eyes.

He knelt on the ground beside me. "This could have been so much easier, *amore mio.* I gave you so many chances."

"To what, marry you? Are you saying if I had, you wouldn't have killed me eventually?"

He shrugged and looked as though he was thinking it over. The fucking lunatic. "Maybe, yes. But if you had agreed to sell Valentini, then we wouldn't be in such an *ugly* predicament."

"You're mad."

He shrugged again and gazed off at nothing. "Perhaps, but I am rich beyond your imagination. The maps I discovered that day so long ago, allowed me to locate many of the Sovereign Order of Malta's buried riches, but none as great as the Medici diamond. In fact, all those combined are unequal to its value. Once I possess it, I can disappear and never be seen again." He turned back to me and dug his fingers into my arm. "Time is up—where did you hide it?"

"Hide it?"

"I warned you before not to play with me, Pia. I saw you. You had it in your hand. Of course, I had no idea what it was at the time. When I read the stories of Estancia Valentini and how she paid off the Italian government but kept her fortune in one stone—the Medici diamond—that's when I realized what you'd found."

"Paolo, I didn't find a diamond that day. The stone I found was red, a worthless bauble."

He looked at me as though he didn't understand what I was saying, either that or I was very stupid.

"I'll show you if you untie me."

"No tricks unless you want to end up like him," he said, motioning toward Georgio.

I reached into my pocket and pulled out the stone.

"*Santa Madre di Dio,*" Paolo gasped, taking it from my hand.

"That's the Medici diamond?" I muttered.

"*Sì.* It is the most valuable in the world. Worth twice as much, at least, than the Hope Diamond. It could bring in seven or eight hundred million dollars. More perhaps." He looked up at me. "And it's all mine." His smile was pure evil, like it had been earlier on the *terrazza.*

"Yours? Don't you mean 'ours,' my love?"

My head spun around like Paolo's did. Standing only a few feet from us was Gabriella, although now she looked more like the woman I'd met in the lobby of the London hotel—Donnatella.

"Of course that's what I meant," said Paolo, rising to his feet.

"Stay where you are!" she yelled, pointing the gun in her hand at him.

"But—"

"Shut up, or I'll kill you first." She motioned with her gun. "Toss it over here."

Perhaps knowing she'd kill him no matter what, Paolo raised his gun instead. I squeezed my eyes closed and prayed to the Holy Mother of God, *Santa Madre di Dio.* I knew that when I died, my baby would too. *"Please forgive me, Mylos."* I heard the popping sound and waited. I could feel Paolo still beside me. I opened one eye.

"Drop the gun, Paolo," I heard someone say.

I looked over my shoulder and saw three guns pointed in our direction but aimed at Paolo.

When he moved his hand just slightly, I knew he was going to fire. I slammed my body against his and then rolled away as fast as I could. At the same time,

I heard the guns fire. I squeezed my eyes shut again, only opening them when I felt Mylos' arms around me. He lifted me up, and I buried my face in his shoulder, not wanting to see.

He held me in his arms, carrying me out of the caves, past Donnatella's lifeless form, past where Paolo had killed Georgio.

28

Grinder

I didn't take her inside; I carried her down the stone walkway that led from the caves to the villa, and then all the way down to the farmhouse. I ignored her protests, telling me to put her down, until she finally gave up and rested her head on my shoulder.

I carried her through the front door and up the stairs, finally setting her down on our bed. She laid her cheek on the pillows, and I rested mine above her belly. Her fingers stroked my hair as I stroked the place where our baby grew inside her. And both of us cried.

My mobile remained silent throughout the night, for which I gave my thanks to Rile. Tomorrow would be soon enough for us to debrief.

Pia was still asleep when I heard the front door ease open. I pulled on my joggers and crept from the room in time to catch a glimpse of Countess Maria walking into our kitchen.

"Buongiorno," I said, walking in behind her.

"Oh, Mylos!" She put her hand on her heart. "You startled me. *Buongiorno.* How is my daughter?"

"Sleeping peacefully. What do you have there?"

She opened the basket she'd carried in and took out fruit and pastries—the same breakfast Pia and I shared almost every day.

"The baby?"

"There are no signs that there's anything wrong."

She closed her eyes, crossed herself, and looked up at the ceiling. I knew exactly how she felt.

"Where is it?" I asked.

"In a safe place."

"I think you're wrong about the curse."

"Perhaps," she murmured. "However, the last man to hold it, died a horrific death."

"Pia didn't die. She held it. I didn't die either, and I certainly should have—more than once."

"How does it feel, knowing you carried the Medici diamond—something worth several hundred million dollars—around in your pocket?"

I laughed. "Is that really what it is?"

"*Sì,* according to the research your colleague did last night."

"What's crazier is that Pia sent it to me in the mail."

The countess' eyes opened wide.

"The first letter she sent me."

"She loved you then."

I nodded. "And I, her."

When the countess looked behind me, I knew Pia was there and had heard.

I turned around and looked into her eyes. "I love you, Pia."

She stepped forward into my arms. "I love you, Mylos."

"I should be on my way," said the countess at the same time we heard a knock at the door.

"Buongiorno," said Rile when I opened it.

"Come in," I said when he was already halfway through it.

"Has the countess shared the news with you?" he asked once we joined Pia and her mum in the kitchen.

"What news is that?" Pia asked.

"Decker was able to find quite a bit of information on the Medici diamond. Although before your illustrious family renamed it, it was known as the Heart of Eternity."

"But it's red," said Pia.

Rile nodded. "The rarest color diamond in the world."

"What else did Decker find out about it?" I asked.

He handed me a piece of paper, which I declined to take, so he handed it to Pia.

She skimmed it and then looked up at me and smiled.

"It says." She cleared her throat. "The blood within the stone grows cold with hate. With love, it warms."

"Is that all?"

She shook her head. "The man filled with hate, shall die of it. The man filled with love, shall live of it."

I looked over at Rile, who held the heart-shaped stone in the palm of his hand. Interesting that the countess trusted Rile enough to think the stone was in a safe place as long as he had it.

Pia took it, walked over, and reached for my hand. She turned it over and set the stone in my palm.

"This is worth an ungodly sum of money, sweetheart."

"Without love, it isn't worth anything."

I smiled and stuck it back in my pocket.

Rile had breakfast with us and then announced he was leaving that afternoon to return to Spain. "Should you need me here in Tuscany, please do not hesitate. Particularly if you require a best man at your wedding," he said with a wink.

I walked him to the door. "Thanks for everything, mate."

He held up one hand in a wave and walked to the SUV. Before he got in, he studied me.

"What?"

He shook his head, got in, and drove away.

"Such a wanker," I mumbled as I walked back inside.

"I'm worried about Nonna Bella," I heard Pia say as I entered the kitchen.

"I am too," said the countess.

Before I had a chance to sit down, I heard another knock at the door. This time it was Mateo and Lucia.

"We just stopped by to tell you we're on our way to Casavetti," said Lucia when I invited them in.

"Pia and her mother are in the kitchen."

Mateo hung back when Lucia went in, so I did too.

"AISE is asking for the whereabouts of the diamond."

"Why is that?"

"Something about it being the property of the Italian government."

"I see." I scratched my chin. "If you were to encourage them to search harder, I'm certain they'll find proof that is not the case."

"I was hoping you'd say that. I didn't want to be the one to tell Zia Maria that I had to confiscate it."

"No, I wouldn't have wanted to do that either," I said with one hand in my pocket.

Mateo held out his hand, and I shook it. "I feel funny thanking you for your help. I told Rile the same thing."

"No thanks necessary."

"Lucia and I have been assigned to recover the missing antiquities."

"Good luck to you."

"Someday I'd like to learn more about the Invincibles."

"And someday, you shall."

After saying goodbye to Lucia and him at the door, I closed it behind them, hoping that was the last of our visitors for today.

When I walked back into the kitchen, both women were quiet. When she saw me, Pia held her hand out to me. I stood behind her and wrapped my arms around her waist.

"Lucia said Nonna Carina spoke to Nonna Bella."

"And?"

"Georgio told her horrible things about us," said the countess.

"I'm sorry to say I'm not surprised."

"With everything that's happened, she decided it best that she doesn't come back to work at Valentini," said Pia.

"How do you feel about that?" I looked between her and her mother.

"Who would she cook for, anyway?" said the countess with a wave of her hand. "Me?"

"You need to eat, Mamma."

"And you think I cannot cook?"

Pia laughed. "Have you ever?"

She folded her arms. "I'll learn."

I doubted there was anything the women in front of me couldn't do if they set their mind to it.

"I'll go and let you have time alone."

"You're welcome to join us for dinner, Mamma," said Pia when they cheek-kissed.

"We'll see," she said, patting her cheek. "It fills my heart with joy to see you so happy. You know why you are, yes?"

"Why, Mamma?"

"Because you're having a girl. That is why."

"No, Mamma. It's because I'm in love."

Countess Maria smiled and winked at us. *"Sì."*

After she left, Pia and I sat out on the *terrazza*. Me in a chair, her on my lap. I rested my hand on her belly.

"I love you, Pia."

She turned her head and kissed me. "I love you, Mylos."

I cupped her cheek with my palm. "This is probably the least romantic proposal in the history of mankind, but I want to marry you."

She smiled and brought her lips to mine. "If you take that stone out of your pocket, I can guarantee that no woman has ever been proposed to with the Medici diamond."

"Would that be a good thing?"

"The blood within the stone grows cold with hate. With love, it warms," she murmured.

"And the man filled with hate, shall die of it. The man filled with love, shall live of it."

***

Over the course of the next few weeks, Valentini seemed to come alive. Elio Cesare returned as head winemaker, and his wife, Nonna Carina came back as both cook and housekeeper, saying with just the countess living in the house, she could easily do both.

The countess offered to let us live in the villa, but knowing how I felt about the farmhouse, Pia graciously declined.

I finally got Pia to accept that, since we planned to eventually marry, my money was also hers.

There was enough of it to do whatever needed to be done at the winery, with plenty left over to start rehabbing the cottages on the property to let to travelers.

The only one off-limits was the farmhouse. I'd told Pia I would renovate it myself, with the help of my father, of course, and maybe even Wills.

I doubted my sister would have a complaint about spending several weeks in Val d'Orcia. Nor would my mum.

Shortly after I put forth the request, my father called to say they'd be on their way in the coming week and that mum had already checked with the countess, who had invited them to stay in the villa with her.

"What about the bombats?" I asked.

"Good name for them," said my father, laughing. "Evidently, there is another house on the property that will suit them quite well."

I wondered which one and asked Pia when my father rang off.

"Nonna Bella's house. Unless you think that's a terrible idea."

"We should pay her a visit." I pulled her into my arms.

Pia's eyes lit up. "Do you think she'd welcome us?"

"I cannot say; however, my prediction is that she would like to make peace as much as you would."

"Yes, well, maybe."

Three days later, armed with the address that Decker had found for me, I went to the village with two things in mind.

First, I would see if Nonna Bella would be willing to see Pia and the countess. Second, I would pick up the ring that I intended to propose with properly.

I parked and walked through the village Pia and I visited so often. As I passed by what she and I jokingly referred to as "our fountain," I stopped and closed my eyes, remembering how she'd looked the day she first spoke to me.

"You like to look," she'd said.

Opening my eyes, I knew straightaway where I wanted to ask her to be my wife.

I walked past the market merchants, who were busy putting away their wares. I turned a corner, took a deep breath when I reached the correct address, and knocked on the door.

"Hello," I said to the woman who answered, hoping she spoke enough English to understand why I was there. "My name is Miles Stone. I'm here to see Bella Rossi."

Moments later, the door opened wider.

"Mylos?" said the woman I'd only met once, over ten years ago.

"Yes. Nonna Bella?"

"*Sì, sì,* come in."

I left an hour later with a very full belly and an equally warm heart.

As I followed my GPS directions to the jeweler, I thought a lot about Rile's words before he left. I knew what I had to do, immediately placing a call to Edge. Too late, I calculated the time.

"Ciao," he answered in a groggy voice.

I laughed. "Sorry to wake you, mate."

"No worries. How are you, Grind?"

"I've never been better. Honestly."

"I know the feeling. Hang on." I heard some rustling in the background and then a door close. "Rebel is still asleep."

"Again, I'm sorry about the time. I can ring you back later."

"No, no. Tell me why you called, Grinder."

"It's about Rile."

"The bloody wanker."

"Right. About that…"

The ring I'd commissioned the jeweler to make was even more beautiful than I dreamed. The perfectly round, four-carat diamond I'd chosen, was edged on either side with five rubies. One for each year I'd loved Pia Deltetto.

29

Pia

"What time is it?" I asked, stretching my arms above my head.

"It's early," Mylos answered, leaning over to kiss my forehead. "Go back to sleep."

"Wait," I pleaded, reaching out my hand when he stood to walk out of the room.

He came back and sat on the edge of the bed, brushing my hair from my face. "You are so beautiful."

"Tell me what else I am, Mylos?"

"Let's see." He brushed my lips with his finger. "You are very sexy."

"Not romantic?"

"Definitely romantic." He nuzzled my neck. "And you smell bloody fantastic."

"You remembered!"

He lifted up the bedclothes and crawled in next to me. "I remember everything, Pia."

I rested my head on his shoulder and put my arm around his waist. "We haven't talked about how long you can stay."

He shifted and turned on his side. "What do you mean?"

"You know, when you'll have to go back to your… other life."

"Hang on a minute." He got out of bed and rushed out of the bedroom.

"Where are you going?" I shouted after him.

"I'll be right back."

"Bring *un caffè!*"

"It'll take too long, and besides, it isn't good for the baby."

"It isn't good for the baby," I mimicked under my breath. I missed coffee more than anything, even wine.

When Mylos came back, he had a bouquet of flowers in one hand and something I couldn't see in the other. All I knew for certain was it wasn't a cup of coffee.

I folded my arms and pretended to pout.

He set the vase of flowers on the bedside table and tucked whatever he had in his other hand behind him when he sat on the bed.

"You asked me a few minutes ago when I had to get back to my 'other life.' For the first time ever, I know exactly where I'm supposed to be. What's more, I never want to leave. You are my life, Pia. You and the sweet little baby growing inside of you." He reached behind him, pulled out a box, and opened it. "Please marry me, Pia."

I covered my face with my hands and cried the happiest tears I ever had. We'd talked about getting married, but I'd wanted to wait until after our baby was born. Until this moment, I had no idea that what I was really waiting for, was for Mylos to ask me.

"Yes, yes, yes," I cried, throwing my arms around him. He climbed back in bed, beside me and put the ring on my finger. "It's so beautiful."

"It's you and me. Ten years."

I studied the ring and thought about his words. It was us.

"I'm not leaving, Pia. I want you to know that."

"What about your work?"

"You mean in the tasting room?"

I swatted him. "Be serious."

He put his finger on my chin, and I looked into his eyes. "I am serious. This is our life. You and me and all the babies we're going to make."

"My mamma told me that since Estancia, each heir has only had one baby."

"Yeah? Well, we're going to break that record. Let's practice right now."

It was mid-afternoon, and we were downstairs, rummaging around for food when the look on Mylos' face turned so serious it worried me.

"I did something yesterday."

"What did you do?"

"I went and saw Nonna Bella."

I sat down. "What did she say?"

"She wants to see you, Pia. You and your mother. She told me her heart breaks every day she isn't here to take care of you."

I smiled through my tears. It sounded exactly like something she'd say. "But?"

He shook his head. "Nothing. When I told her how much you and the countess missed her, she cried and cried."

"Did she say anything about Georgio?"

"A little. She blames herself."

"She shouldn't."

"She said he'd always had a chip on his shoulder about their life. No matter how many times she told him she was happy working for your family, he would chastise her for not wanting more."

"I asked my mamma once about Georgio's papà. What she said sounds a lot like Georgio. He left them, wanting more out of life, she told me. My mother that is; Nonna Bella never spoke of it."

"Do you want to go and see her?"

"Of course!"

"I mean now, Pia."

"I would like nothing more." I stood and wrapped my arms around my dear husband. He wasn't yet, but that's the way I thought of him. "I love you, Mylos."

"And I love you, Pia."

"When should we get married?"

"Tomorrow?"

<h1 style="text-align:center">30</h1>

Grinder

I stood at the front of the little chapel that I'd never known was on the Valentini estate. Seated in the pews in front of me were my family—my parents, my sister's husband, and their three bombats.

On the other side of the aisle sat Countess Maria and, next to her, sat Nonna Bella. Behind them were Elio and Nonna Carina, and behind them were the Casavettis. Other than Mateo, I couldn't tell the cousins apart. I knew one was Antonio, one Francisco, and one Vincenzo. Their father, Giuseppe, who insisted everyone call him Joe, was crying as much or more than Nonna Bella was, just like Zia Renata was, beside him.

"I told you he'd do that," said Mateo, who stood on the other side of the man I'd asked to be my best man, Cortez "Rile" DeLéon.

Edge had told me the day I called, that as much as he wanted to be at the wedding, he couldn't be away from Rebel. I understood in the same way he understood why I wanted to ask Rile to stand up with me today.

Decker couldn't be here either; Mila was due to give birth to their baby any day now.

"How are you, my friend?" Rile asked as the music began to play and I saw Lucia standing at the back of the church.

"Never better."

He put one hand on my shoulder and brushed a tear away with the other. "You deserve this and every happiness."

I thought back to the day I asked him if he'd be my best man. It was one of the only times I remembered him being at a loss for words. And then he asked me why. I explained that if it weren't for him meeting me at the hotel that day, I wasn't sure I would've believed I could have the life I did now.

As Lucia began her walk down the aisle, I saw my sister, Lily, come and stand in the same place. When our eyes met, I knew that, like with Rile, if it weren't for her, I may never have seen my beloved Pia again after that first time, when we were both sixteen years old.

"I love you," I mouthed, and she did it back as she began her walk.

And then…I saw Pia. She stood alone where Lucia and Lily had stood before her. She'd insisted she wanted to walk down the aisle alone, and now I understood why.

She wore a simple sleeveless white dress that hugged her growing belly. Her eyes met mine, and she smiled.

The music changed, those in the pews stood, and Pia took a step toward me. Her simple bouquet of flowers hung at her side, as she danced and sashayed her way to me. Her eyes were bright with happiness, and maybe a little mischief. My heart almost burst with love.

If we could go back in time, I bet we'd see Estancia look just like Pia did today. Two powerful women, like those of every generation in between, capable of accomplishing anything, capable of changing the world, yet the most important thing in their lives was love.

We spent our honeymoon at the farmhouse, getting it ready for the rest of our lives. Each day, my family would show up to help, as would the countess, the Casavetti cousins, and their parents. At night, we'd walk up the hill to the villa, where Nonna Bella would have a feast prepared for everyone.

Pia would grow tired, and she and I would sneak off, sometimes going straight back to the farmhouse, and other times, stopping first to swim and make love in the moonlight.

The day our baby girl decided she was ready to meet the world, wasn't much different than any other. We were surrounded by our family, talking more than working on the farmhouse, when Pia's water broke.

My father rushed up to the villa to get Nonna Bella and Nonna Carina. Three hours later, they and Pia's mother looked on as my baby girl was born into my arms.

"Just like my Pia," said the countess through her tears. "In such a hurry to make her mark on the world."

I looked into my wife's eyes as I handed her our precious bundle of joy. I had no doubt that my daughter would change the world in any way she wanted to, but most importantly, like her mother, she'd changed me. Without their love, I couldn't imagine living another day. I reached into my pocket and pulled out the heart-shaped stone that was worth so much more than anyone knew. Not in the millions the world might value it, but in the love and life it represented.

Epilogue

Grinder
One Year Later
Val d'Orcia, Italy

Today, we were back in the small chapel where Estancia Valentini Deltetto Stone would be baptized in front of the same family and friends that were with us on our wedding day—plus a few more.

Our beautiful baby girl, who looked so much like her mother, was blessed with two sets of godparents—my sister and her husband, and Edge and Lucia.

Pia worried the priest wouldn't allow it, but Maria assured her he would. "We're Valentinis," she'd said, and my wife nodded.

My best mate, Edge, was here today, with his wife, Rebel; Decker was here too with Mila and their baby. The only person not with us was Rile.

I found myself feeling melancholy in his absence. "He's a wanker anyway," said Edge, bumping me.

I laughed. "How'd you know I was thinking about Rile?" He pointed at my bottom lip that I was brushing with my index finger.

"Bloody hell," I muttered and then sheepishly looked about to see if anyone heard me. "He was here for the wedding."

"Sorry again we couldn't make it, mate."

I shook my head. "You're here now."

"She's beautiful," said Edge, looking over to where my wife stood holding our baby girl.

"They are."

"I'm happy for you, Grind," said Edge, squeezing my shoulder. "You're a different man."

I shook my head. "I'm the same man. I was only different when Pia and I weren't together."

"Hello, my friends," I heard at the same moment another hand clamped my shoulder.

I spun around and awkwardly hugged the man who had become a dear friend. "You made it. Welcome."

"There is someone very special I'd like you to meet." Rile put his arm around a very beautiful woman—one I recognized. "Gentlemen, may I present my…"

Keep reading for a sneak peek
at the next book
in The Invincibles Series—
RILED!

1

Riled

When I close my eyes, your voice floats through the jet's white noise and settles on my heart like a cold mist. And then you're gone. Always gone before I can make sense of the words you so desperately want me to hear. I stop short of crying out for you to say it again, beg like I always do, for you to stay with me and never leave.

I wait for the pain as it claws its way back into my soul. There's comfort in the familiar. At least I know I can feel…something. My eyes fill with unshed tears, and I murmur your name. *Celestina.* More than my northern star, you were my sun, my moon, my universe, my guiding light. Without you, I'm lost. So lost.

Forcing my eyes open, I look out the plane's window as we begin our descent to Mallorca, the island that has become my home because it's where you rest and will, for all eternity.

I stayed in my seat while the Bombardier taxied from the private runway to the hangar it shared with the much larger planes the DeLéons kept at their disposal. Part of me wished I could tell the pilot to turn around and take me back to Italy.

I stood, stretched my legs, and peered out another window when I saw my valet pull the black 1963 Mercedes-Benz 190 SL out of the same hangar where the plane would sit until the next time I needed it. I smiled when he lowered the top; it was perfect convertible weather—sunny but not too hot. Mid-May truly was the best month on the island.

I took one step down the plane's ramp when I was overcome by what felt like a hurricane-force gale, yet the air was completely still. I gripped the railing with one hand while I rubbed my temple with the other as the message came through, loud and clear.

Kensington is in danger.

About the Author

USA Today and Amazon Top 15 Bestselling Author Heather Slade writes shamelessly sexy, edge-of-your seat romantic suspense.

She gave herself the gift of writing a book for her own birthday one year. Forty-plus books later (and counting), she's having the time of her life.

The women Slade writes are self-confident, strong, with wills of their own, and hearts as big as the Colorado sky. The men are sublimely sexy, seductive alphas who rise to the challenge of capturing the sweet soul of a woman whose heart they'll hold in the palm of their hand forever. Add in a couple of neck-snapping twists and turns, a page-turning mystery, and a swoon-worthy HEA, and you'll be holding one of her books in your hands.

She loves to hear from my readers. You can contact her at heather@heatherslade.com

To keep up with her latest news and releases, please visit her website at www.heatherslade.com to sign up for her newsletter.

MORE FROM AUTHOR HEATHER SLADE

BUTLER RANCH
Kade's Worth
Brodie's Promise
Maddox's Truce
Naughton's Secret
Mercer's Vow
Kade's Return
Butler Ranch Christmas

WICKED WINEMAKERS FIRST LABEL
Brix's Bid
Ridge's Release
Press' Passion
Zin's Sins
Tryst's Temptation

WICKED WINEMAKERS SECOND LABEL
Beau's Beloved
Coming Soon:
Cru's Crush
Bones' Bliss
Snapper's Seduction
Kick's Kiss

ROARING FORK RANCH
Coming Soon:
Roaring Fork Wrangler
Roaring Fork Roughstock
Roaring Fork Rockstar
Roaring Fork Rooker
Roaring Fork Bridger

THE ROYAL AGENTS OF MI6
Make Me Shiver
Drive Me Wilder
Feel My Pinch
Chase My Shadow
Find My Angel

K19 SECURITY SOLUTIONS TEAM ONE
Razor's Edge
Gunner's Redemption
Mistletoe's Magic
Mantis' Desire
Dutch's Salvation

K19 SECURITY SOLUTIONS TEAM TWO
Striker's Choice
Monk's Fire
Halo's Oath
Tackle's Honor
Onyx's Awakening

K19 SHADOW OPERATIONS TEAM ONE
Code Name: Ranger
Code Name: Diesel
Code Name: Wasp
Code Name: Cowboy
Code Name: Mayhem

K19 ALLIED INTELLIGENCE TEAM ONE
Code Name: Ares
Code Name: Cayman
Code Name: Poseidon
Code Name: Zeppelin
Code Name: Magnet

K19 ALLIED INTELLIGENCE TEAM TWO
Coming Soon:
Code Name: Puck
Code Name: Michelangelo
Code Name: Typhon
Code Name: Hornet
Code Name: Reaper

PROTECTORS UNDERCOVER
Undercover Agent
Undercover Emissary
Coming Soon:
Undercover Savior
Undercover Infidel
Undercover Assassin

THE INVINCIBLES TEAM ONE
Decked
Edged
Grinded
Riled
Smoked

THE INVINCIBLES TEAM TWO
Bucked
Irished
Sainted
Hammered
Ripped

THE UNSTOPPABLES TEAM ONE
Furied
Merried

COWBOYS OF CRESTED BUTTE
A Cowboy Falls
A Cowboy's Dance
A Cowboy's Kiss
A Cowboy Stays
A Cowboy Wins